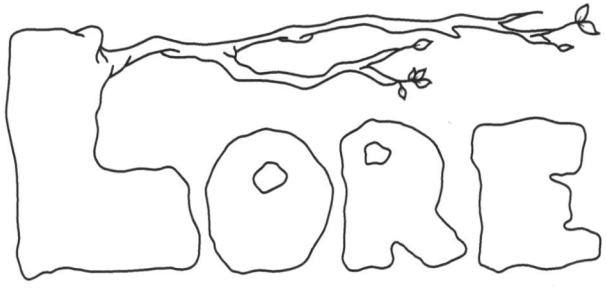

vol. 2 · no. 4
November 2013

Edited by
Rod Heather and Sean O'Leary

Published by The LORE Firm, LLC
Haddonfield, New Jersey

www.lore-online.com

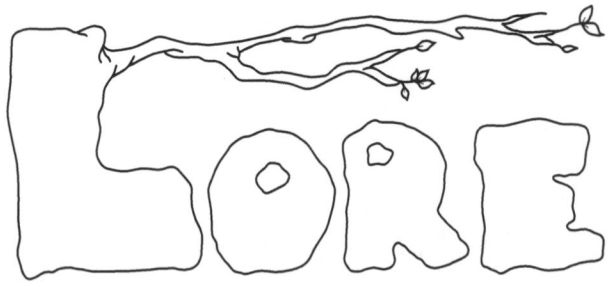

vol. 2 · no. 4

EDITORS / PUBLISHERS
Rod Heather & Sean O'Leary

CONTRIBUTING EDITOR
John R. Platt

ASSOCIATE EDITORS
Doreen Cavazza
Scott Emerson
Cynthia White

COPY EDITOR
John Picinich

LORE: vol. 2 · no. 4 — November 2013
Published by The LORE Firm, LLC, Haddonfield, New Jersey

ISBN: 978-0-9847730-5-3

© 2013 by The LORE Firm, LLC

All stories are copyright their respective authors and no portion of the text may be reprinted without their permission.

Cover artwork "Invocation in the Temple of the White Centipede"
© 2013 by Axel Torvenius

"At Your Own Risk" © 2013 by The LORE Firm, LLC

For contact information and submission guidelines, please visit:
www.lore-online.com

Printed and bound in the United States of America

10 9 8 7 6 5 4 3 2 1

INNARDS

At Your Own Risk v
Sean O'Leary

THE DEVIL IN RUTLEDGE COUNTY 6
Tory Hoke

THE SATURDAY DANCE 22
Ted Mendelssohn

LICKING THE HONEYPOT 34
Steven Mathes

HAVEN 45
S.D. Kreuz

BENEATH THE LOVELIEST TINTS OF AZURE 66
Jeff Samson

ROBOT TIME MACHINES AND THE
FEAR OF BEING ALONE 78
Rebecca M. Latimer

FIMBULWINTER 86
J.J. Irwin

ON THE MAKING OF A DEAD MAN'S HAND 100
George R. Galuschak

GHOST 119
Bear Weiter

Dramatis Personae 127

Invocation in the Temple of the White Centipede
Cover artwork by Axel Torvenius

At Your Own Risk

Upon entering the Temple of the White Centipede, this issue's cover artist Axel Torvenius tells me, we must be sure to step quickly into the circle. That nasty-looking character on the right is not an usher! Our hostess is doing all she can to maintain the barrier, but in order to leave, with both our hide and sanity intact, the proper words must be intoned and the correct frequencies achieved. Now, where did I put the leaflet that pasty, hollow-eyed acolyte handed to me at the door? Oh, right, I dropped it into the first brazier just outside the foyer! No wonder he snickered at me. Still, it provided a wonderful aroma... must have been spritzed with essence of myrrh (or is that you?) Well, keep close, perhaps this striking volume here on the lecturn will provide some insight.

LORE 4. Hmm... sounds intriguing. Let's have a look, and don't let your fingers get too close to our dark visitor over there. My, he does look hungry, doesn't he? Not for food, though, I don't think. You know, I seem to remember seeing something like him a field guide somewhere, probably not Audubon... maybe Calvino... or Barlowe? Anyway, I think we're safe as they only feed on souls. Oh, you have one? Well, then, we better find the incantations quickly. I'll tell you what, you read through this rather handsome collection of what promises to be macabre and exiting tales and I'll check what's on for lunch in the cafeteria. Oh, I should remind you that the admission fee is non-refundable.

Good luck!

Sean O'Leary

THE DEVIL IN RUTLEDGE COUNTY
Tory Hoke

It was my fault. It happened 'cause I prayed to the Devil.

Of course I prayed to God first. I prayed every night since I realized Pa was a drunk.

Not a joker or a hothead or a layabout — a drunk. I prayed God would make him quit drinking. I prayed God would turn him back to the easy-laughing man who took us fishing on Saturdays.

I prayed whenever I heard Pa retching in the backyard at dawn.

I prayed whenever the constable's boys dragged him home at midnight.

I prayed when Essie got bit on the heel by a copperhead, and Pa was face-down in bed, and there was only one other person we could turn to. I carried poor Essie, groaning and sweating, to the Tybee Inn, where straightaway Mrs. Tybee sent her maid Cecilia for the doctor, and she tucked us in her green velvet parlor and gave us each a butterscotch, though we were both too sick and scared to eat 'em.

Pastor Price got there first, which scared me bad, but finally Dr. Watts came to stick a needle in Essie's arm. I heard the three whisper together. Pastor Price said "it's in God's hands" and Dr. Watts said he'd done all he could, but Mrs. Tybee kept saying, "Those poor girls... those poor girls..."

Mrs. Tybee, with the soft body and bushy hair that smelled like lavender. It was Mrs. Tybee who always overpaid for cheese from our goat, Rambler. It was Mrs. Tybee who asked after our schooling. It was Mrs. Tybee who invited us to Christmas dinner every year, even after Pa quit letting us go.

Dr. Watts took us home. Essie felt well enough to eat her butterscotch, but I kept mine in my top drawer on a stack of a dozen other gold wrappers, and I asked God to bless Mrs. Tybee even if He didn't see fit to bless us.

I laid Essie on her bed and propped her with the quilt Ma made her. I dabbed her forehead and changed her bandage and brought her water. It was a hot August and dry as tinder.

She'd curl up like paper if nobody saw to her.

When Pa stirred awake mid-morning, I told him what happened. He cried over Essie and begged her forgiveness; she had to pet him to calm him down. He was so tore up he went to the kitchen to open a bottle. I couldn't take it. I grabbed his sleeve and pulled.

"Pa, no!" I said.

He grunted and pushed me. I pushed back. His bottle hit the floor and spilled. Pa yelled and shoved me into the kitchen table. I whacked my head. My eyes watered and I checked for blood, but Pa just stared at me with those swollen yellow eyes. He had a round hard gut like a watermelon under his shirt. His hands shook. He looked like a man twice his age.

"I'm gonna go wash up," he said, and he picked up his half-empty bottle and shambled out.

God had turned me down.

I took Ma's cross from the wall and threw it in the corner. I found Ma's Bible on her desk and I banged it on the table 'til the pages bent.

LORE

I hollered "God damn! God damn!" until Essie hobbled out, all scared and sad-looking. I told her to get back to her room.

Then I kneeled down and prayed. I could hear Pa huff and the water pump squeak outside.

"Dear Devil," I prayed. My heart thundered. "You're all I've got."

The pump squeaked and Pa huffed.

"Fix him," I said. "Fix my Pa."

Silence.

I felt goosey all over. I ran to the window. Pa stood at the pump with his back to the house. He had his feet spread and his back stiff and his hands stretched behind like he'd been socked in the kidneys.

I ran outside to him. Sun blinded me. He flickered in and out of view. My hand caught his sleeve. He loosened up and turned.

"What is it, darlin'?" he said.

He still looked like Pa, mostly. But his belly was flat. His eyes sat deep in his head like a sober man's, but too bright, like sun that bounces off water and gives you a headache. He smiled at me, but it was a wrong smile. It was the smile you make with a knife in your teeth.

"Pa?"

"Dear Mary," he said. He handed me his bottle. "Why don't you take care of this for me?"

I took it. Then across the yard I heard a screaming like a woman's. I looked up and Rambler was bleating and banging her head against the fence.

Not-Pa looked at her with small concern. "What's got into her, I wonder?"

The noise drew Essie onto the porch. She saw Pa and squealed. "Pa!" Not-Pa scooped her up and kissed her cheeks. Our goat kept screaming. "You're up!" laughed Essie.

"I am," said Not-Pa.

"What's wrong with Rambler?"

"Funny old goat," he said. He touched Essie's blue-black heel. "Little girls need shoes. Let's go to town."

"Yes!" said Essie.

Not-Pa reached for my hand. "Shall we?"

My gut told me to run, but I didn't. He smelled like honeysuckle and lemon. He couldn't be all bad. I took his hand. It was cool like the tile in the Tybee Inn.

The whole half-mile to town he carried Essie. Men we passed seemed half-sized. I felt like I did whenever I waited for Pa in a bar full of smoke: sick, but giddy. Taller than the world.

. . .

Our first stop was the tavern. The drinking men flinched away from us. It's rude to bring kids drinking. It reminds.

A worn-out looking woman in a yellow dress came up to us.

"Howdy, Bill," she said. Her voice rasped like ash. "These your girls?"

"Not today, Sugar," said Not-Pa. "But tomorrow. I got a proposition."

"All right," she said. She winked and left us.

Not-Pa ordered: "Whiskey."

The bartender shook his head. "Bill . . . "

"Just one more." Nearby, a bent-up young man in a clean suit laughed in his glass. "What's so amusing?" Not-Pa asked him.

"I didn't say a thing," said the bent-up man.

"A drink for the laughing man, too," said Not-Pa. "And a milk for my girls." He spent every coin in his pocket.

The bartender served us. Not-Pa passed the bent-up man his drink. Me and Essie and Not-Pa and the bent-up man toasted each other. Not-Pa emptied his glass and sucked his teeth.

Then he turned those too-bright eyes on me and pushed his glass away. That was a first.

Essie downed her milk. She leaned to Not-Pa and whispered, "Can we go? It smells bad in here."

"Of course," said Not-Pa. He rose, the steadiest I'd ever seen him come off a barstool.

The bent-up man lurched sideways as we passed. Not-Pa caught him, planted him back on his chair and brushed off his coat, saying, "Easy there."

He took us down an alley to the back of the tavern where a half-dozen sweaty men were running a dice game. They recognized Pa and gave him mean-eyed smiles.

"Dollar game, Bill," warned one.

"Understood," said Not-Pa. He reached in his pocket and pulled out five dollars he hadn't had before. "Room for one more?"

I knew we'd be here a spell. I took Essie's hand. There was already some other man's kid sitting on a crate nearby, drawing in the dirt with a stick, so me and Essie sat with him and helped him draw.

Not-Pa came to Essie and put the dice under her nose. "Give them a blow for me, angel," he said. She did. He winked at me. The alley went queasy. Warm milk backed up my throat.

He threw.

· · ·

We headed out of town with new shoes on our feet, a doll for Essie, a wooden puzzle for me and crackling bags of saltwater taffy. Not-Pa carried a side of pork on one shoulder and a cornmeal sack on the other. He didn't sweat a drop.

Essie danced in her new shoes. "They're hard!" she said.

"They'll break in," said Not-Pa.

Someone caught her eye. "Mrs. Tybee!" she shouted.

I looked and Mrs. Tybee was strolling with Pastor Price alongside us at a distance, watching. She startled at her name but put on a smile. Not-Pa headed straight for her, startling her even worse. She took a step back. Pastor Price held firm.

The Devil in Rutledge County

"Good to see you, Bill," said the pastor. He was bald and ruddy and smelled like liniment.

"Mrs. Tybee," said Not-Pa, shaking her hand. "I thank you for taking such good care of my girls."

"You . . . you're welcome, Mr. Yadkin," she said.

"There's been some changes in our house. I hope they never need such good care again."

Mrs. Tybee went rabbit-rigid. "They're always welcome," she said, looking at us girls to make sure we heard. "No matter what."

"You're a kind soul, Mrs. Tybee," said Not-Pa. "Daresay the Devil wouldn't waste his time on you!" He looked at Pastor Price. "Of all people."

"Will these changes bring you and the girls to church?" asked Pastor Price.

"We'll see!" said Not-Pa. "Good day!"

He led us away with a spring in his step. I looked back. Mrs. Tybee watched us with a hand on her heart while Pastor Price talked and talked.

Near sundown, at the edge of town, a pack of nasty boys chased a dog past us. Essie and I knew these boys. We shrank behind Not-Pa, but they saw us anyway. One nudged another and they smirked together, but they kept running. Only one ragged boy with a missing tooth lagged behind; this was Ray Bridger, my age but smaller.

"Goat face! Goat face!" he called. Fifty yards away if he was any, he called again in case I hadn't heard: "Go-o-oat fa-a-ace!"

Not-Pa turned on him. The kid froze. Not-Pa whisked up a hand and Ray Bridger caught three feet of air and sailed chin-first into the dirt: a bony pile, one elbow sticking up wrong. I clutched Essie.

"What happened?" she asked. She'd missed it somehow.

The wind ruffled Ray's hair, but he didn't move. He could have been just a bundle of sticks. I stopped. Not-Pa and Essie didn't even break stride.

"Is he all right?" I asked.

Not-Pa looked back and shrugged. He looked different. His cheeks were hollow and baggy.

LORE

I didn't go to Ray. I know I should have. But I was afraid.

When we got home, Rambler was gone. Her rope was broken and two planks of fence knocked down. No sign of her besides. I looked at Not-Pa, and he shrugged again.

"She was always funny, wasn't she?" he said.

Essie was asleep before she hit the pillow. I couldn't stand to wake her, to make her wash her face and brush her teeth, so I tucked her in. I crawled in bed beside her and stared at her rosebud mouth and those long, long eyelashes. I lay there until the urge to make water got me up.

I left Ma's cross on the bed for Essie.

I found Pa walking down the porch steps.

"Where you headed, Pa?" I asked.

"Stretch my legs," he said. His voice rasped. His face looked pinched and papery. His nose bones stuck out. "Where you headed?"

"Outhouse," I said.

"Don't be long."

"You either." I watched him head for the creek.

I did my business fast and ran back to the house. I grabbed Ma's Bible and flipped through it. It had small advice: Jesus said, "Get thee behind me," and that was enough for him. I couldn't tell what would work for little girls from Rutledge County.

I searched for Not-Pa through the kitchen window. Curiosity nagged at me. I took the carving knife and followed his trail to the creek.

I walked quiet as I could. There was just enough moonlight to see and be seen. I heard Not-Pa before I saw him: splash and hiss, splash and hiss. I edged into the brush, so dry it scratched, and kept low.

There he was, knee-high in the water. He was man-shaped, but dried out and gaunt, a smokehouse carcass of a man. He cupped water over his pearly skull and back meat the color of clotted blood. Up went a wallop of steam that smelled like fried pork.

My heart beat so hard it rocked me. I edged closer.

Then I saw the tail, coiled around Not-Pa's right thigh, squeezing and stretching like a separate living thing.

The vomit urge hit me. I tipped my chin up to fight it off. Then I noticed above me a flabby yellow shirt dangling from a tree limb. Coarse black hairs on the sleeves. Five skinny sacks on each cuff. A long slack hole ran through the hood. Over that, tucked in yellow flaps, those glaring, too-hot eyeballs.

A Pa-skin suit.

I did vomit then. Thank God Not-Pa's splash and hiss drowned out the sound. I picked up and ran to the house as fast as I could.

I camped myself on our bedroom floor with knife and Bible and back to the door. God knows how I ever fell asleep. But I woke to bacon and egg smell with Essie standing over me.

"What're you doing?" she asked.

"He ain't Pa," I said.

"Of course he is! Mary, you're so dumb." She started to butt me out of the way. I hauled her back by the arm and she gave a yell. The kitchen sounds went quiet. My gut flipped.

"Essie, I need you to do me a favor," I said.

"What for?"

I took Ma's cross off the bed. "Take this," I said. "Keep it in your pocket. All day. All night. Will you?"

"What for?" she said, more suspicious.

"A favor," I said. "Please, Essie." I dropped the cross in her skirt pocket and held her close. She smelled dirty. We both did. "I'll make it up to you."

"Fine. Now let me go!"

I did. She bounded down the hall calling, "Pa! Pa!" I heard him scoop her up. With my knife, I followed. Not-Pa was polished and sleek and honeysuckle and lemon again. Even over a hot stove there wasn't a drop of sweat on him.

"Mornin', girls," he said. "Afraid I can't stay long. I got work to do in town."

"Can't we come with you?" whined Essie.

"Not today, sugar," he said. "You two gonna play nice together?"

"Yes, Pa," said Essie.

Not-Pa looked at me. "Mary?"

"Yes, Pa," I said.

But as soon as he was out of sight I told Essie she could have anything she wanted if she'd let me go to town without telling. Essie hemmed and hawed and in the end she took my bag of taffy.

I ran to Mrs. Tybee's. When I turned up on her step sweaty and wild, she clutched me and searched me for harm.

"I'm all right!" I told her.

"Essie?"

"At home. She's all right, too."

Mrs. Tybee took a deep breath. She shooed away Cecilia and brought me into the parlor. "What is it, Mary?" she asked. She sat across from me and stared into me with those big, loving eyes. Suddenly I knew I couldn't tell her. I couldn't tell her it was my fault.

I fell to my knees and hugged her waist. Her skirt was cool and smooth. She smelled like lavender. It seemed selfish to cry, so I didn't.

"My sweet child," she said. "My poor, sweet child." Her voice caught. I was making her suffer. "What is it?"

"I did something bad," I said.

She sighed relief. If she only knew! "What happened?"

"I can't tell you."

"You can tell me anything."

"It was so bad. I can't."

"You're just a little girl." She picked up my chin. "You can tell me. I will understand."

I couldn't stand the weight of so much love. I had no practice with it. I shook my head.

She gave me time to reconsider.

"Whatever it is, Mary," she said at last, "You must make it right as best as you are able. Anyone can make a mistake, but a good Christian makes amends. All will be forgiven, I'm sure."

I nodded. Of course she was right. Only I had the power to fix things. Then I remembered.

"Have you heard anything about Ray Bridger being hurt?" I asked.

She shook her head. "Not that I know of, dear. Should I?"

"No. No, I hope not."

I hugged her again, as tight and as long as I could.

Then I went straight on to the church to find Pastor Price. The rector met me and said he was away and could I call again? I said I would come back tomorrow. I had no choice.

On the way out I passed the Tybee Inn again. I saw the tavern woman in the yellow dress lounging on the porch, laughing with a man in banker's stripes. She didn't look worn-out anymore. She wore jewels and a fox stole, and this yellow dress was an evening gown. The sight of her made my skin creep.

Essie had gotten sick on the sofa. Too much taffy. I told her to wash while I cleaned the sofa as best I could, and she felt so guilty she went without arguing. Boric powder left a light spot. When I heard Not-Pa climb the stairs I hid it with a blanket.

Not-Pa looked pinched again. His cheeks had fallen. Red rims showed under his eyes. He carried a brown paper bag with something the size of a cat squirming around inside.

"You girls have a good day?" he asked.

"Sure did. Essie's washing up."

"Good girls," said Not-Pa. "Why don't you fry us up some dumplings? I have some work to finish."

He headed out back with his squirming paper bag. I saw him reach a hand behind his neck and readjust his crinkled skin.

His borrowed skin.

After Essie — neat and pretty and full of dumplings — fell asleep, I waited for the sound of the front door. When I heard it, I checked for Ma's cross. Essie must have put it under her pillow. I put it back in her pocket. Then I got the kitchen knife and I followed Not-Pa's trail.

There he was in the creek again, bathing his twisted-up body. There was his red snake tail, climbing up and down his thigh. I hid myself in brambles and worked my way until I was under it: the yellow skin-suit. I stretched the knife upward. WIth one eye I watched the man thing to see if he would feel it.

I sliced one fingertip of the hanging skin, from knuckle to tip.

The thing didn't notice.

I crawled back to the house before my luck could run out.

I ran through the sitting room and shut myself in our bedroom. I crouched behind the door and listened for Not-Pa to come back in. In due time there came the slow pound up the steps and the creak of the front door. Footsteps came in. They headed straight for our room. I held my breath. He waited there, just on the other side of the door. I heard his tail scrape up and down. I didn't dare move. I didn't dare breathe. I stared at the doorknob, waiting for it to turn. I heard a sliding sound like a palm against the door. Then Not-Pa clucked his tongue. Three times. Tsk, tsk, tsk.

The footsteps moved on. Pa's bedroom door open and shut.

I breathed again.

Shaking in every muscle, I opened the door. I peered up the hall and saw nothing but darkness. So I shut in Essie and sat outside our bedroom that night, knife in hand, back to the door. It wouldn't do to be surprised.

I didn't sleep a wink.

· · ·

Pa's bedroom door clicked open at dawn. My heart jerked. Not-Pa came out and stared at me. There was a bandage on his finger.

"Good morning, Mary," he said.

"Good morning," I said.

He grinned. Then he did a funny thing. As he went to the kitchen, he twisted his neck like an owl so all the while his eyes were on me. It made me sweat.

He made more eggs and bacon. The smell got Essie up. She didn't look right. She was clean and fed, but there was something pinched about her face now, too.

"Pa," she said, straight to whining. "Can I come with you to town today?"

"What for?" asked Not-Pa.

"Ray Bridger's got a brother bad as he is. I want to see what you do to him."

"What would you like me to do to him?"

"Knock him down." She mashed her eggs as example. "Squeeze his head. Make his eyeballs pop out."

"For you, sugar?" he said. "Anything. But tomorrow." He kissed her forehead, and their starchy skin scraped together.

Not-Pa left. This time I didn't have to bargain with Essie to get away. She stayed at the kitchen table and filled all our butcher paper with bloody drawings of what she wanted Not-Pa to do.

· · ·

I found Pastor Price having tea. His office was dark as the inside of a goat, and everything creaked. He had me sit and offered me a cookie. It tasted like old closet.

"What's the trouble, Mary?" he asked.

"Pa's got a devil in him," I said. "I need you to help me get it out."

"That's very serious," he said. His voice ran up and down. "What makes you say that?"

"His eyes ain't right. He's up to strange business. And he takes his skin off at night, and he got a red thing like a snake around his leg."

Pastor Price blushed, but he leaned back all satisfied. "Ah, Mary, that's a normal thing," he said. "You see men and women have different parts, and your father's no exception . . ."

He went on but I was too mad to listen. Did he think I'd never seen a dog hump? Or a bull do his concern? Didn't his own son corner me and try to show me his thing last Fourth of July? But I just cut eyes at him and said, "If he's always had it, how come I never seen it before and now I see it every night?"

Pastor Price turned gray and I was sure I'd got to him. But then he said, "Your father has turned himself around. He's rebuilding himself in the community. In the church. It would be a shame to ruin him now." I went red hot but he kept talking. "I can have a word with him, if you like."

Me, ruin the Devil! I bit my tongue. I'd learned what I came for. Pastor Price wasn't gonna help me but by accident. He talked and talked and eventually he asked me to kneel with him and pray, and I did. But when he closed his eyes I kept mine open.

When I headed home I knew what I had to do. It was him or me.

Not-Pa came home with another rustling bag that he took out back and dealt with. We had a peaceable dinner. Essie showed us her drawings, and Not-Pa seemed to like them. I smiled plenty, but I kept my eye on Not-Pa and he kept his eye on me.

At night I waited up and listened for the front door to squeak. Right around midnight I heard Not-Pa leave.

I gathered up Ma's quilt. I counted to ten and I shook Essie's shoulder. She was sleeping with a screwed-up face like an old woman. "Quit, Mary," she said.

"Essie, I'm gonna do something and I need your help."

She scoffed and rolled over. "I helped you enough . . . "

"This is important. This is very, very important."

"What?"

"I'm going out. I need you to bolt the door behind me. Pull the drapes and don't look out or go out 'til dawn. You understand?"

She slit eyes at me. "I ain't doing that. You don't like him. I do. Do what you like, but I ain't helping."

That rocked me. I told her, "He'll come for you . . . "

"He won't hurt me. Worry about your own self."

That scared me bad. She turned her back on me.

I took a lantern and wrapped Ma's quilt around it to block the light. Outside the air was scalding and the crickets screeched. I left the door unbolted. I had no choice.

I padded down to the creek. From fifty yards I could see him, a zig-zag man. No skin on.

The creek steamed. His tail shifted.

The skin was hanging on a different branch this time. He'd learned. Now it was just a foot behind him. Some animal crackled through the brambles and he swerved at it to listen. I ducked in a thicket. His eye sockets were empty, but something in the back of them sparked.

Satisfied, he went back to bathing.

Fifty yards to the skin. I got down on my hands and knees. I tucked the lantern bundle under one arm and slowly, too slowly, I crawled through the brambles to him. I got on my belly when I had to. Thorns raked me. Even through the quilt, the lantern burned me. My muscles twitched. I'd wait for a breeze to hide my noise and I'd surge ahead a foot. Sweat ran off my nose.

I got to the end of the brambles, six feet from the creek's edge and the skin hanging over it. The thing stood six feet from that. I had to be fast. I had to be certain.

I worked the quilt loose around the lantern, making room for it to slip out. I grasped the handle. I pulled up to a crouch.

I waited. The Devil stretched his crooked limbs. Then he bent to the creek one more time.

I sprang! Open air! I caught the skin by the hands and whipped it into my arms. Not-Pa whirled and swung. I ducked; his finger-bones scratched my shoulder. He came for me. The water bought me seconds. I ran back a yard, threw down the skin and swung up the lantern. He lashed at me again. I clouted his hand. He laughed.

I cried, "Stop or I burn your hide!"

He drew back to his full height and glared. In each empty eye socket was a tiny flame.

"Not mine," he said. His voice was high and rustling like a locust. "Just borrowed."

"It doesn't matter," I said. "Do as I say or I'll burn it."

"Oh? And what do you say?"

"I want you to go."

"Is that all?" He waved a hand. "Just wish it, little girl, and it will be so."

"And bring my father back."

The Devil cocked his head, very pleased with himself. "He'd be the same as he was," he said. "That's what you want back?"

"Yes."

The Devil shrugged. "You need only wish for it."

I stared at him. He only grinned, flashing every tooth in his head.

"I . . . I wish for my father back," I said.

The Devil laughed 'til he yelped. "Sad effort. No, Mary. You have to wish for him back as hard as you wished for him gone."

My heart thudded. I looked down at the yellow skin. Pa's smeared-up face looked drunk.

"Shouldn't be so hard," said the Devil. He wagged a finger at me. "You're his own flesh and blood, aren't you? He's your Pa. He raised you from a baby. He bounced you on his knee."

That struck me. I hit my knees and sobbed. The Devil got eager and crawled to me on all fours. His tail swished.

"You can't, can you?" he said. "He had another week at most, and the bad memories would have died with him, and you and Essie could have gone to Mrs. Tybee with pure hearts. But no. You couldn't wait. Will you ever tell your sister what you've done?"

I cried 'til I choked. My tears turned cold and greasy.

"Ah! There it is." said the Devil. "That's what I came for." He cupped his hands under my chin. I didn't stop him. I wanted to die. He caught my tears and licked them. "There it is. Innocence . . . There's nothing better . . . " He used some language I didn't know, and then just the sound of locusts.

"I wish you were gone," I said.

A clapping sound, right in my ear, and the Devil vanished. Under my hand lay Pa's body — his true body, back inside his skin — stiff and yellow and swollen as three days dead.

There on the path, kneeling in dirt, stretched over Pa's body, I cried myself out of tears.

At last I dressed Pa's corpse. It was slow work, and it hurt, but I buttoned his shirt and sat him against a tree and folded his hands. A little dignity. I could give him that.

I took the quilt and lantern, hiked back up the hill to the house. I hoped I would never get there. But I did, and Essie was waiting in the sitting room. She had her own quilt tight in her arms. Round cheeks and rosebud mouth again. She threw her arms around me when I came in.

"Mary, where were you?" she cried. "I woke up and there was nobody here!"

I held her and I buried my face in her hair.

"Pa's dead," I told her.

She stared at me with those big angel eyes. "Pa's dead?"

"He drank again and drank too much and he died."

She didn't move at first. Then she crushed up her face and arched her back and wailed like a baby. I held her tighter. She sobbed herself into hiccups.

"It's not fair!" she said.

"I know."

"We were just starting! Everything was just starting..."

I whispered that it would be all right. I whispered about Mrs. Tybee. I held her as long as she needed.

I would let her believe I was good. I would keep the secret for two.

THE SATURDAY DANCE
Ted Mendelssohn

When the Baron died, he died alone.

There was no one to lead him under the ground and over the ground and onto the road that leads under the waters, for who would dare guide the guide? Had he not traveled that way himself, many times and over, taking the good and evil, the wise man and the fool, the husband and the wife — but not the children, for they were under the protection of Papa Ghédé, who knows what jokes are unfit for the young — all to the land of Guinée, to await rebirth or to come again as Ghédé themselves?

But when Baron Saturday died, he had no one to help him.

"This is most unexpected and most vexing," said the Baron. Except, of course, that Baron Saturday is quite crude, so what he really said, in the *Kreyol* of his childhood, was "Fuck me blind! I'm fucking dead!"

The Saturday Dance

Then "Where are my companions?" he asked rhetorically. Except the Baron will only use the word "rhetorically" some fifty years after the Bon Dieu himself retires, so what he really said was "Lakwa! Kriminel! Papa Ghédé! Get the fuck out here, you cock-sucking, blue-assed monkeys!" And he meant it, for the Baron is not subtle.

But his fellow Ghédé did not come. At this, the Baron thought that perhaps his wife, Mama Bridget, who had hair of fire and a tongue like a razor, had scared off his boon companions and decided once again that she would no longer tolerate his whoring, or his parties that lasted weeks, or the large black cigars with which he perfumed the fine marble mausoleum that was her home.

But if that were true, Mama Bridget would have been waiting for him, bottle in hand, to offer him a drink of rum with hot peppers, or to break the bottle over his head, depending. And she was nowhere to be seen.

All he saw was the dark ground, and the midnight sky, and the faint rim of light that runs like a band around the horizon of the *Peyi Lonbray*, the land of shadows. And there was not a house light to be seen, nor a *banda* song to be heard.

The Baron fingered the nine stones on the band of his top hat, and the nine twists of the hangman's knot he used for his bow tie, and sat down on a boulder with curious *vévés* carved into it, and he pondered.

Now the Baron did not do this willingly, for he is no Simbi or Ogou — he is a Ghédé, and although he is monstrously clever, and can dance the moon to sleep and the sun into the sky and get the Earth itself with child, thinking too deeply makes his head ache. But soon enough he came to his first conclusion, which was "I am in bad trouble."

And then he came to his second conclusion, which was "I will never again gamble with a crafty *bokor*."

And then he came to his third conclusion, which was "Or at least, not while I am drunk."

For the *bokor*, the sorcerer Agri, had summoned him by all the rites of Voudoun, and invited Saturday to a feast in his honor, with all the Barbancourt he could drink and all the fine island girls he could fuck, and what Loa spirit, even a milk-blooded Rada, could refuse an offer like that?

So Saturday was well and truly screwed. But being a Ghédé, and the best of them, by damn, he did take time to laugh at his own predicament.

"You are one damn fool, Baron Saturday," he said to himself, chortling all the while. "You ride the sorcerer's body like a horse, at his own invitation, no less, and then he waves a spirit bottle in front of you, and . . ."

And here the Baron trailed off, because he himself did not precisely remember what the sorcerer had done. What was in that Barbancourt he had drunk, anyway?

Well, no matter. He knew that he was dead, again, even though death is a tricky thing for the Loa, and he knew where he was, at the crossroads. And if there was one place that was Saturday's, it was here, at the gate between the churchyard and the road, the sand and the sea, the moon and the black horizon. Here was his power, and here he could call whom he would. First of all, the sorcerer.

He rummaged in his pockets, and laughed a short, sharp "Ha!" when he found what he expected, a cow's hoof. At the feast Agri had never let the Baron shake his hand, because Saturday takes with him whatever he has hold of. Instead, trying to be clever, the *bokor* had offered Saturday the hoof, and hoped the Baron would ignore the childish deceit out of politeness — but the hoof itself had belonged to Agri, and for a Ghédé Loa as powerful as the Baron, that would be enough.

So the Baron traced the outline of a grave in the earth with his skull-topped walking stick, and the grave opened wide. He dropped the hoof into the dark, moist soil and closed the grave again. Then he pissed upon it, muttering all the time, and walked three times around it. Then he rapped the stick upon the ground and yelled "Come up, you shit-stained bitch! Rise!" And on the third repetition, the ground shuddered, and there was a moan from the dirt, and Agri sat up with cotton in his nostrils and his lips sewn shut and a confused look on his face.

"Even dead, I still got it," laughed Baron Saturday. "Right, motherfucker?" And he ripped the binding from Agri's lips so he could speak.

When Agri had finished screaming, the Baron questioned him long and earnestly about the rite he had performed.

Now the details of the rite, and the meanings behind it, and the *vévés* used, and the drum beats chosen, these are all things that no man knows, because the Ghédé do not want it to be known, and never will, and the Ghédé can be hotter even and more hasty than the Petro Loa when it comes to the mysteries of death and rebirth. This is as it should be, because after all the rum and the parties and the fucking and the music, the Ghédé balance death and life, and no one may interfere with that.

But what the Baron did learn was almost enough to make him sober. For after the *bokor* described the wherefore and how of what he had done, the Baron himself, the Saturday Man, the King of the Graves and the Children, could see not a single way out.

Saturday's power on Earth was broken. He would never again be able to return as a *bawon*, possessing the willing, protecting the dead, fucking the women until they walked bowlegged, or healing the sick and the victims of witchcraft. No matter how fancy his top hat, how snappy his dead-man's suit or smiling-skull rings, the dead would no longer recognize him as their guide. Even here at the crossroads, his powers would soon fade, until he was no more than a civilian, another mortal soul bound for the world below the waters.

But when he asked who had taught Agri this rite, and why, the sorcerer could do no more than shrug his shoulders, no matter how terrified he was.

"Well, I need a drink now," said the Baron, after he put Agri back in the ground. But there was no *piman* to be found, no Barbancourt, not even the cheap rum they serve to tourists mixed with fruit juice and sugar.

LORE

The Baron glanced at the horizon. His power would wane with the moon, but until it set, he was still the mightiest of the Ghédé, and he would know the truth of things.

Before the *bokor's* feast had killed him, Saturday would have just yelled a name, and his Ghédé would have appeared, cursing, shouting, abusing him in the vilest terms, but always, in the end, obedient. Now, the Baron had to draw signs in the earth and sing and kill chickens like a priest. It was humiliating.

But he did it, and sure enough, out of the shadows sauntered Ghédé Nibo, long ivory walking stick a-dangle from his wrist, long black riding coat a-drape around his shoulders, long cigarillo a-puffing from his lips.

"Well, look who it is," purred Ghédé Nibo, "Oh, Father Saturday, you look like shit."

"And don't I know it," grunted Saturday. "Now shut the fuck up and give me to drink."

Ghédé Nibo handed Saturday the bottle of white rum and medicinal herbs he carried always, and the Baron drank it down.

"So, my son," said Baron Saturday, wiping his lipless teeth, "still fucking boys?"

"Every night, father."

"Well, pitch, don't catch. Who killed me, my son, and why?"

"Father, I cannot say, and that I tell you thrice."

"Well, what can you tell me, boy, before the moon sets?"

"I can tell that I saw my mother weeping. I can tell that Baron Kriminel always speaks the truth, even if it is just a scream. And I can tell that everything between the grave and the cunt serves a purpose, even if I do not know precisely what."

"You are a good boy, Nibo. You will defend the infant dead?"

"Always, my father, and I shall be a voice for the voiceless spirits who have not gone below the waters."

"Then you are a true Ghédé, and I bless the day we adopted you."

The Saturday Dance

Saturday always grins, but he grinned extra wide at Nibo, and Nibo faded back into the shadows. Then Saturday stood and stretched his bones until they rattled and cracked, and summoned the next Loa.

Baron Kriminel appeared with a shriek, his bag of heads bouncing on his belt, an army of *zombis* at his back. Even taller and leaner than Saturday himself, Kriminel leaped like a jaguar, bony fingertips clawing at Saturday's eyes.

Saturday stepped back, dropped to one knee, and brought the head of his walking stick up into Kriminel's crotch. Kriminel fell, shrieking, and Saturday took a running start, and kicked him in the face. He leaned down and pulled the bag of heads from Kriminel's belt and waited.

"Still your boss, bitch," said Saturday, "Until the moon sets. Should I kick you again?"

Kriminel whined though bloody gums and clutched for the bag. Saturday dangled it just out of reach.

"Speak up, *pinda*," said Saturday. "Who set you on me? Who set Agri on you?"

Now Baron Kriminel is the legbreaker of the Ghédé. He collects the debts owed to them on the second of every November, and not even Baron Saturday will fuck with him for too long. But Saturday had wondered many a time how so stupid a Loa, even for a Ghédé, kept all the debts straight in his head before the *Fet Ghédé* each year.

So Saturday kicked him again, and again, and one more time, and rolled Kriminel over on his side, and went through the pockets of Kriminel's long coat of skins (never you mind of what) and Saturday found what he expected to find — a creased black handbook filled with names and dates.

Then he kept the book and kicked Kriminel away into the shadows without it, and that is why, to this very day, some foolish *voudouisants* think they can beg favors of the Ghédé and hope to be overlooked come the *Fet*. And each year, they discover their mistake.

LORE

So the Baron sat on the crossroads stone once more and read through the ragged handbook. It was filled with names and dates, and many pertinent facts about his fellow Loa, bright facts and dark. Saturday was interested indeed, for these facts could cement his place among the Ghédé, and the Ghédé's place among the Loa, if only he could escape what was coming. But he had only until the moon set, and the handwriting was cramped and crabbed, and the secret signs and *vévés* in the book were enough to make even Saturday's head ache, so he paged ahead looking for a clue to his current predicament.

Then he found what he feared he would find, and he chuckled again, for he was a fucking Ghédé and he would laugh at anything. But his laugh had a melancholy sound.

For the third time Saturday called on a Loa. But this time he did not summon, and he did not drum, and he did not sacrifice like a priest, because a man does not cast a spell or lead a service for his own wife. Instead, he built a bonfire and called his wife's name.

"Brigitte! BRIGITTE! Get your ass out here, you milk-white, blood-haired bitch!"

And sure enough Mama Bridget stepped out of the flames, pale and red-haired and green-eyed, but with her usual sharpness tucked away, like the blade of a pocket knife.

"Hello, Saturday," she said calmly.

"'Hello' my ass," said the Baron. "Like we're strangers on the street, woman? Why did you kill me?"

And Mama Bridget looked down.

"I knew it," said the Baron. "Why else would your name be in Kriminel's book! Was it that waitress in Port-au-Prince?"

"No."

"Those twins in Pétionville, with the big tits. You got angry over them."

"Don't be silly."

"I told you, woman, I *like* you skinny. Big tits I can get anywhere."

"It wasn't a woman, you foolish man!" she cried in vexation. "You think I can't find some man of my own when I want to *konyen*?"

The Saturday Dance

Saturday's eyes widened behind his dark sunglasses. "That field hand in Baton Rouge! I knew it!"

"Yes, yes."

"And that taxi driver whose sister had the mighty ass. And that skinny student on the team at university, I bet you did it right on the court!" He stepped closer to Maman Brigitte, towering over her, and his shadow spread out behind him.

"Tell me, woman..." he glared down at her. "Did he have a bigger *zozo* than me?"

And Mama Bridget laughed, even through her bottle-green eyes were red and puffy, and then they were in each other's arms.

After a fair while, when the Baron had tucked himself back in, and Mama Bridget had rearranged her skirts, the Baron looked up at the sky, and he saw the moon dwindling to the horizon.

"The time is coming, woman," he said. "Don't let me die in ignorance."

Mama Bridget nodded, and then she was a true queen of the Ghédé, hard as stone, fierce as night, fertile as black grave soil. "I killed you, my love, because nothing lives forever, not even the Loa."

"That's a lie!" he said, before he could stop himself. But even as he denied it, he remembered the thousand thousand times he himself had said the same thing to the men and women on their final trip to Guinée. He had said it as consolation, but had he truly meant it? He was Ghédé, after all. They might mislead, or trick, or dupe, but no Ghédé would outright lie about death and life.

"No," he said. "It's true. I just never thought it meant me. Did I not die once already? Have not all the Ghédé done so?" He sank onto the stone, amazed once more. "How could I forget that? Was there a spell? Am I mad?"

Bridget sat next to him and stroked his bony cheek. "You forgot because you had to forget. To lead the Ghédé, to dance the *banda*, to travel the road to Guinée and back, over and over again, to face grieving children and bereft parents, how could you remember their sorrow, feel their pain? For a year you would be the greatest of all Loa, beloved for your compassion; and for another year you would struggle to do what was right; and in the third year, weighed down by the sorrows of others, seeing decay and the corruption of flesh from moonrise to moonrise, you would go mad. And a maddened Loa is a terrible thing."

"I hear the wisdom of it," said Saturday, "but I don't feel it."

Mama Bridget nodded. "Because you did not remember. And now you will." She touched his forehead gently with one finger, and Saturday remembered.

He remembered toiling in the fields, cutting sugar cane under the equatorial sun. He remembered the moments of pleasure with his woman, his mortal woman, and the joy of seeing his first child, even though she was a girl. He remembered the long years of fear, struggling to earn enough food, to keep his daughters safe from the *kannay* and his sons from the thieves and *asasens*. Standing over his sons, determined that they learn their letters so their lives could be better. Seeing all the work, all the life, washed away on the back of a great storm, and being an old man, used up at thirty-four. He remembered being killed while blind drunk by the *bòs* during an argument, shot dead by a man on horseback.

He crumbled to the ground, weeping, and he knew that Bridget was right. She crouched over him, stroking the smooth bone of his head where once there had been hair and flesh.

"Papa Ghédé chose you because you were a good man," she said. "Because you had spent your life afraid, but doing what was necessary. You would never be a Baron Kriminel, or a smoothie like Lakwa, uncaring and untouched. And you deserved some time to be happy before Guinée."

Saturday laughed loud, a laugh that sounded like a gasp. "Yes, woman, because I am so damned happy now."

"Your *cimetière*, where you were the first man buried, was destroyed by the great earthquake," she continued. "So your time as a Baron had ended. We sent the *bokor* to distract you, and did what was needful. This was never to be your final resting place."

The Saturday Dance

Saturday sat up slowly and clutched his head, for he was now both mortal spirit and Ghédé, and the clash between the two was like snorting a handful of pepper flakes the day after a drunk.

"So now I go on to Guinée?" he said. "What happens there? Is it paradise? Hell? Or just a fancy word for nothing at all?"

Bridget shrugged. "How do I know? My time is not yet. I am here to carry out the laws of Ghédé, and they say your time is up."

Saturday stood. It was a hard thing, to see your life whole, your sorrows like a millstone, your pleasures nothing more than a handful of pennies in recompense, and then to walk alone to a place that you did not even know. He ran a hand across his face, half expecting the dark, creased flesh that had once been his, but feeling only the bone of a Ghédé.

And with that, he remembered being the Baron. He remembered the dead with whom he had walked, joking with the men, flirting with the women, breaking the stiffness of even the most pompous so that they were laughing and grinning by the time they reached the road's end. He remembered them all, their names and faces, the farmers and fishermen, mothers and peddlers, potters and mambos and nurses and scoundrels, whether worn out by care or rejoicing on the way, but always happy to have someone to talk to. He remembered breaking hexes, and saying "I will dig no grave for you" to the victims of witches and *bokors*, and turning the bad intentions of the priests of the left-hand way back against them. And below the self-satisfaction of the Ghédé, beneath the pain of his mortal years, he felt grateful.

Walking alone was a damned hard thing. But maybe he could do it. And maybe, really, he was not alone.

Baron Saturday stood straight and laughed. "Will you come with me a ways, woman?"

Bridget looked down. "No."

Saturday grinned. "Well, piss on you then." He stretched his arms wide and his voice ran through the dirt like an earthquake. "What about you, my brothers and fathers, cousins and sons? Lakwa? Nibo? Brav Ghédé? Who will walk with me? Any of you?"

He waited for a moment. The night gleamed with eyes, and was filled with rustling, as of a thousand thousand patent-leather shoes, scuffing shamefully on the wooden floor of a dance hall — but nothing else.

He turned slowly to face all of them, degree by degree. "I was born Eawin, in the land beyond the waters. And then my name was Jean in the fields. And now my name is Saturday. But what I am is Ghédé! SO FUCK ALL OF YOU! UP YOUR ASSHOLES! WATCH ME WALK, BITCHES!"

He grinned wide at all of them, and blew a kiss at Mama Bridget. He raised his right hand and said "I'm going to need my fucking rum!"

And Papa Ghédé, short and dark, in the tallest top hat of the family, walked out with a prime bottle of Barbancourt, in which 21 of the hottest peppers in the islands had been steeped. He handed it to Saturday, pulled him down, and kissed him on both his bony cheeks.

Saturday raised his left hand and said "And I want a better pair of sunglasses, you fuckers!" And Mama Bridget handed him a beautiful pair of Ray-Bans, with the left lens knocked out, because the Baron now saw with the eyes of Man and Ghédé. He kissed her once, with plenty of tongue, and grabbed her ass, and the Ghédé yelled and hooted and whistled. Then he shoved her away and straightened his coat.

"Now give me my fucking cigar. Make it a Presidente!" And Nibo came out with a lit cigar and said quietly "I will walk with you, my father."

Saturday said "You take one step with me and I'll kick your ass. You've got boys to fuck and work to do!" And he shoved Nibo away as well.

Then he extended his long, bony finger and swept it across the Ghédé like a fire hose, and said "Where I'm going, you all will be! I'll see you in Guinée, bitches!"

The Saturday Dance

Then he snapped his fingers, and from the last of his magic, the *banda* music started to play, and Baron Saturday did the Pelvic Thrust and grabbed his crotch all the way down the road to the Land Beneath the Waters.

LICKING THE HONEYPOT
Steven Mathes

They call me Gramps. My girlfriend goes by Martha, and maybe that's her real name. That's between her and me. I'm a badass, she's a badass. We have an exploit all ready to launch, but of course someone's always watching.

Badass? This was never meant to be. The kids? They never thought to transform me, old Gramps, into a cyber-criminal. They care nothing about us old people. Store us and forget us.

I live on a capsule warehouse. A tenth the cost of planet-side nursing, though no legal limit on rejuv. The capsule takes care of bodily functions. It feeds me when I'm hungry, fixes me when I'm broken. It locks me in here forever, with nothing to do.

What were they thinking? Sorry, but I have ideals.

"Hi, Gramps!" says my girl.

"Hey, lady," I answer.

"I think we're almost ready."

Licking the Honeypot

Martha and I knew each other flesh-side. Before we went to our separate capsule warehouses, we sort of had this thing for each other. Out here in old-fart orbit, we finally hooked up.

Her kids think I'm after her money. My kids think she's after mine. Not to worry, we do indeedy-do plan to spend! We've always wanted more than a tourist's life.

Martha's capsule is in a warehouse over French Guiana. Mine is in one above Singapore. The weightlessness is key. Easier to get that VR total immersion. Latency is minimal, but it still gets in the way of lovemaking.

It's better when we meet on middle ground, log onto a server halfway between us. Then the sweetly-symmetric latency is about the same for both of us. We plan to own that little spot. Physically. That's the exploit.

Everyone up here who isn't brain dead sooner or later gets caught sneaking through a bank or a government office, learning things about congressmen or other big shots.

Never mind exactly how I got busted, except to admit the files belonged to law enforcement. I was compelled to cooperate, work in computer security, or have my capsule cut.

It took me a year of playing along while secretly learning hacks, doctoring my arrest records. I found some things about some career politicians when I was exploring, but I had to play it just right. You can get kids and politicians to do all sorts of things if you play to their egos. Finally, I forged a couple of work transfer documents, and got myself back into retirement.

"Gramps? Wake up Gramps!" says a male voice.

I authorize this covert line from my grandson. At least it's encrypted. Family is family.

"Jimmy? Is that you?" I whine. "You're not going to take me out of here, are you? And why can't you text?"

"Take you out of there? Text? Don't talk like that. We wouldn't just stick you in orbit to get rid of you! Or if we did, at least we'd feel guilty."

LORE

"Kids . . ." I mutter. "Do you even know how to text?"

Jimmy laughs. I trust Jimmy more than the other kids, because at least Jimmy can laugh.

"Gramps, I need your signature."

"For what?"

"A release, so I can move your money."

"You want my money?" I say.

"You asked me to do it, remember? I promise you won't notice if I steal some."

"You need a signature — because I can't sign for stuff in here? Does that mean you're trying to get me out of this capsule?"

"Stop, Gramps. I paid for an electronic witness this one time, just to get things rolling."

"A witness? I suppose you expect me to reimburse you?"

"No! I'll just steal it from you later. But you have to open up your home directory. Do you know how to do that?"

"Give you my password?"

"No, no, Gramps. Never do that. Just lower your firewall."

Lower the firewall? These kids are so helpless around technology.

I have a fake directory, a little honeypot for pests like Jimmy's electronic witness. The witness is spyware, they always are. The kids trust them, and then they're surprised when they start getting flooded with junk. A witness? Not much different from a virus.

I lower the firewall to the honeypot, but keep my real home tight. A honeypot, a deception, a fake set of personal secrets. Just like the government did to me when they caught me snooping.

"Did I do it?" I plead.

"You did great, Gramps. The witness confirms. But I have to go now."

"Always predictable."

"Yeah, especially now that I've got your money!" he laughs.

"Well next time — please text?"

I cut the connection quick. I delete the honeypot. Then I go back out to be with my girl.

36

Martha waits in multi-media mode, made up in swirling green-yellow sparkles, nothing else but curves. What a body! No kid would ever have her taste in picking the perfect shape. Her avatar has only slight enhancement, looks like her in the flesh, minus a few decades. Or so she says.

Me? I take her into my arms, and in spite of the latency issues, we really dig the feeling, dig smelling the sugar sparkles that go in and out when we breathe each other.

"All set?" I ask.

"I like him. I trust him," she says.

"He'll do," I say. "I wish he'd learn to text."

But there always has to be another interruption . . .

"Hello?" says a female voice.

Just like that, taking a call. Alas, I know that voice.

"You're not my daughter!" I say.

"Mr. Griffin! I'm Special Agent Simmons. Remember me? I dealt with your case when we found you in our secure logs. I thought we had an understanding."

"I keep my word, young lady. I honored it, didn't I? My records are all in order."

"That's the trouble. They are. But I had nothing to do with it."

"Why is that my problem, missy?"

"I don't like being put in a position where restoring your records would make me a criminal. I take it personally."

"Everything is legal and in order, documented and certified. A judge signed off on it. Believe me, the judge had good reason to sign it, you understand? Are you threatening to tamper with legal records?"

"Tampering with evidence and legal records carries huge penalties, sir."

"Exactly, young lady."

"Listen, buster. I'll be watching."

She's just calling about the records. I tell myself that's good news because it means she only just noticed. I know this Simmons. She'll show her hand.

LORE

I go back to my girl.

"You hear that?"

"How could I miss it? She didn't even use a secure line."

The open line is suspicious. When it comes to computer crimes by us geriatrics, she's the one-man show. She knows her tech. Or maybe she just hates old people.

"You think it's a set-up? Notice she didn't mention you?" I say.

"She hates me!"

Martha's daughter is the judge that got us off, a reasonably honest judge except when it comes to her mother. She fixed Martha's problem, which really pained this Simmons.

But now I see.

"It's a set-up," I admit. "But would you change our plan either way? After this much work?"

"What the hell. Let's get this started."

We go musical. I float in pure emptiness in front of half a dozen multimedia streams. Just pure, colorful, abstract data singing in a vacuum, waiting for me to sing back.

We go as low-level as we can and still work fast. I could open a genuine command-line window in an emergency. Go physical in my capsule, feel the pinch of my life support, wiggle my fingers on a slimy keyboard. Oh yes, I have a keyboard. But our strength is the singing. The consoles are good for overrides, for crises, but too slow for real work.

First job? A place to live, our little love nest. Second job? Transportation. A shuttle for each of us to get our capsules to their designated docks in the aforementioned love nest.

Orbital transfer ain't cheap, but space stations are.

My boy Jimmy should have moved the money by now, made a bid, won the auction. Our love nest is an abandoned U.N. mining pod. Don't get me started on government waste, except to say this is prime.

Extra-large external docking bay, heavy-duty expansion bay, mil-spec-hardened core fuselage. The repair logs show that it's cherry. The kids would never understand the sweetness of a hardened mining pod.

Licking the Honeypot

No, don't get me started on waste, but there's thousands of these orbiting here around Earth, around the Moon, wherever. You usually don't get to choose the one you want, you just get to pay your money. But we've got access to the server. All we need to do is change a couple of serial numbers on whatever they gave Jimmy. They pick 'em by random anyway.

"All done!" Martha sings. "She's legally ours — and as soon as the bureaucracy gets around to it, we'll have the title."

She is so sexy when she sings.

"Let's celebrate!" I say. "Let's take a little sex break."

"We have to stay focused, love."

She's right. I'm such a guy. Now there's the transportation issue, which is trickier, along with provisions.

Jimmy's got money in place for that, basically a serious chunk of our retirement, and we're not poor.

However, with Agent Simmons lurking down in flesh-side, we have to do this in secret.

This isn't as crazy as it sounds. There's a black market for kids trying to relocate their elder loved ones to cheaper warehouses, or even to have them "decay into low solar orbit" for inheritance purposes. Oh, there's plenty of firms willing to haul us.

"He did it!" Martha says. "Let's hope it works."

It goes much too smoothly.

The contractors schedule us for pick-up, almost like they were just waiting for the order. We have maybe a day.

Take a break? We rush to buy and ship provisions, rush to get prescriptions to knock us out, buy a drive module to move our future love nest to a safer location.

Chores. I hate chores.

It turns out that adventure is a lot of work! We pull an all-nighter, whatever that means up here. Kids, with their routine, would never understand.

Then we knock ourselves out. Literally. I mean, who would want to spend hours floating in gel, with nothing but your own thoughts — listening to air go in and out of the tube in your throat?

We knock ourselves out, and sleep through the biggest adventure of our lives. It feels so phony, in a way.

But we sleep, and then we wake up. Proud new homeowners.

"Lady? Are you there?" I say as I go online.

"Gramps?"

Her avatar flickers into view, looking pained. I feel my own pain, a hangover from the sleepers. We oldsters may be a bit in love with drugs, but that's life.

"I hurt," I say. "I'm worthless for thinking."

"Something's wrong," she says. "I've been looking around. Our access to the servers is cut. Are we in the right place?"

"We're alone?"

"So far."

I sing myself onto the station's computer. I go straight for the serial numbers, the identification. It all checks.

But Martha speaks true. I find lots of stuff blocked. I sing at it. I can't get through. I keep trying, thinking I'm good, but this is tight. We used to hang out here, used to have free run.

"Simmons is just not that smart!" I whine.

"A trap. A honeypot."

We've been busted. All we can do is wait, the way busted badasses always have, since the beginning of time.

On one level, I don't like being busted, but it feels so good to be a badass. Of course, the call comes:

"Mr. Griffin! Special Agent Simmons again. Remember?"

Audio. Well at least that still works. When The Man needs it, probably everything works.

"So's that all we have? Audio?" I say.

"My, my. You do cut right to business," she says.

Right now I just hate all kids.

"Mr. Griffin. Are you pouting?"

"This isn't fair!" I say.

"You broke the rules. You thought you could just move into a vacant space station, shack up with your fluff?"

Something she said. I send a little feeler to Martha, a little electronic glance of the eye to tell her to stay quiet. She does the best singing, but I do the social engineering.

"It was just sitting there," I tell Simmons. "Nobody cared about it, nobody was using it. We're just borrowing it."

"It's not your property. That's stealing. I warned you."

"But we have rights!"

"Here in government, one hand doesn't know what the other's doing. Sometimes it takes personal attention to make sure justice happens."

"We demand a judge!"

"I wish I could bring you down, place you in a wheelchair in some Little Happy Meadows, but instead I'm pulling a fast one. The station you squatted in was ready for a mission. The crew's already on the way."

"But there's nothing out there! It's the boondocks."

"You get to be explorers."

"Alone. Offline."

"No, you'll have supervision. They think you're computer experts, which I suppose you are. I told them you have a criminal past, but then again so do most of them. How do you think we staff these missions?"

"So we aren't leaving right away?"

"I suggest you say goodbye to your kids. You have audio. I think we can safely give you that."

She laughed as she disconnected. So immature.

I go back to my lady, who needs cheering up. I can't help but smirk.

"What?" she says.

"She doesn't know we bought the place. Like she said, one hand of government doesn't know what the other's doing."

Martha probes, always persistent, always obsessed with solving a problem. I think about contacting Jimmy, but I'm afraid they'd be listening. I don't trust my encryption anymore. So mostly I watch my lady and learn.

I tell you, she's hard-core, way beyond what any kid "expert" could do. In a worst case, we'll gain control of the station sooner or later.

But mostly, both of us are scared. We feel the drive module clank into place a day later. And then, its audio time again.

"Mr. Griffin?"

"Who are you?" I said.

"Captain Rowell. Ready for docking."

"You're docking?"

"That's what I said. You didn't think you'd get that place all to yourself, did you?"

He's so jovial. I hate kids.

"You have the whole crew?"

"Crew and provisions, both."

He sounds like such a young guy. And there's hardly any warning. A clank, and we hear the docking mechanism whir. There's a loud hissing.

"Those are provisions," the captain says. "It'll take some time. While you're waiting, you might want your mail."

Mail?

All of a sudden, our connection opens up to their shuttle, like we're back in the bandwidth, for just a moment. A flood of sparkles, a flood of data. I scan. Martha scans.

"Here's the deed!" I tell her.

Jackpot. It takes me a second to remember the account key, back when I gave Jimmy the money, but I have it. I feed it to the message and the attachment opens up like a flower.

"Passwords, I see lots of passwords," my lady says. "Keys to our new house!"

The passwords work. They open up the servers. We have control.

"What's happening?" said Captain Rowell.

"Just keep pumping, but stay down," Martha tells him. "Stay down, and nobody gets hurt."

Stay down and nobody gets hurt. I always wanted to say that. I hear myself laughing, sounding like Blackbeard.

Provisions, more than we ever needed. We let the bots offload, until they figure out we're taking their food and medicine. As soon as they abort, we cut them loose. We're good for a couple of decades.

"I'm sorry," I say. "You can check, but this is private property."

"You're pirates!" Rowell shouts.

"No, we're the owners. Everything's perfectly legal!"

"No! Pirates!"

I refuse to take much stock in the babbling of idiots. I cut them off once and for all.

And we're back in the bandwidth. We're still in tight orbit, still nestled in data. The sparkles flow and sing and glisten like grains of fine sugar, but we have to hurry.

We don't want to hurt anyone, especially helpless kids. We play it safe. We wait for the shuttle to drift to safety before we activate the propulsion, get ourselves moving. We have fuel to take us anywhere.

Now that we know Simmons will try to cut us off, we build back doors, secret connections to the data. Thousands of them. Then millions.

"There's bunks on this station," I say.

"Are we thinking the same thing?" she asks.

"I can't wait to get into Simmon's home directory, but there's something else I'd like to get into. Face-to-face, with you," I say.

"Ho, ho, ho!"

I begin draining my gel. I hear the pumps bringing me flesh-side. I feel my online presence fading. At last, we're mostly legal, mostly free, and way too much work to prosecute.

It's time to party!

At first I'm scared when I discover Martha has not followed. Then I plug back in to check, and it makes me laugh. She has reinforced our security, built layers of data weaponry. We are now armed to the teeth! I watch, and it's only when Martha has finished that I laugh again. We bought milspec — milspec vessel, milspec servers, and she's brought us

LORE

to milspec on the firewall. I am still laughing, laughing for real when I go flesh-side.

The last thing she did was raise the Jolly Roger.

HAVEN
S.D. Kreuz

"Immortals don't die, that's why they're immortal," Stone said with a slight roll of his glass eye.

"Tell that to him." Rika sent the stack of photos scattering across the ice table.

Stone breathed a thin stream of mist, his good eye remaining locked on her face as he formed a pyramid with his fingers. She pressed her palms onto the cold surface, leaning over the slab.

"If someone's experimenting with my work, I want to know about it," she said.

"You're on the edge, Ms. Rika." He snapped an icicle from the table and began to scratch words into the solid surface. "Things happen to humans on the edge."

"Things happen when immortals show up dead too."

"You mean the tsunami?" He flexed his fingers. "Just coincidence."

"And the firestorm?"

"Unfortunate." He released the icicle. It floated in the air between them.

"Look at this." She tapped the closest picture. "He's had his heart ripped out. The last thing we need are heartless —"

"Ms. Rika." He poked his glass eye and forced it to look at her. "Do you have a family waiting? A pet, even?" His lips stretched into a thin smile as she narrowed her eyes. "Perhaps you should tend to them and leave this in the hands of professionals."

"Professionals, or you?" She peeled her hands from the ice and propped them on her hips.

"You're neither a hunter nor an immortal. I am both." He snorted mist, gesturing to the door. "Leave the hunt for those born to do it."

Rika jutted her chin as she stalked out of the chamber.

· · ·

"So how'd it go, doc?"

Rika glanced at Ben who leant against the glass wall. The toothpick he chewed on almost dropped from his mouth as he smiled a set of jagged teeth.

"How do you think?" Rika said. Ben pushed himself from the wall and rubbed his clean-shaven jaw.

"The boss being helpful as always?"

"That's why you don't have an immortal as head hunter," she said as she stepped over his tail that jutted from the back of his jeans. He shrugged and stabbed his hands into his pockets.

"We need his skills."

"What you need is someone who cares about the welfare of the lower level humans. Immortals never have. If they did, things wouldn't be the way they are now."

"Damn, Rika." Ben spat the toothpick. It missed the frozen rug and stabbed upright in the concrete. "You know better than to talk like that."

"You're a hunter. I don't expect you to understand."

His face creased. "I understand you plenty, but the last thing you want is a mark on your head for —"

"For telling the truth?" She glanced at his tail as it arced behind him like the head of a cobra.

"For telling your version of the truth." He flicked his tail. The fur bristled and it lowered. "You know the rules. I don't want to see your name on my list in the morning."

"Immortals are turning up dead. If this continues, there might not be a morning." She looked out the glass wall at the cracked roads and charred debris. He followed her gaze. She jumped as a column of fire exploded from the black sky and struck the glass. Fire spread along the surface and dissipated. She glimpsed the disinterest in his eyes.

"You're safe here in Haven," he said. She shook her head.

"Nobody's safe in Haven."

• • •

Rika peered at the pyramids that circled the ruined city. The glass walls were clearest on the lower levels where people rushed about. On the next few levels, doors woven out of the elements flickered, as tailed hunters disappeared through them.

She lifted her gaze to the point of the main pyramid. The walls of the higher levels were blacked out. She drew back, spotting a familiar face through the glass.

The immortal threw off his leather coat as he appeared through an ice door in the opposite pyramid, brushing frost from his toned arms. The mark on his left cheek wriggled like a worm beneath his skin.

Rika's stomach gripped as the immortal pressed his face against the window, his eyes locking on her from beneath a pair of spectacles. He smiled and stepped forward. The glass liquefied before her. She shuddered as the fresh whisper of snow swept through the room and the immortal stepped out of the wall before her.

LORE

"Have you been well, Doctor Grey?" the immortal said.

She dug her nails into her palms as the immortal peered at the wall. The glass shifted into a mirror.

"You've messed with the original signature, Michael. Mattershaping is dangerous," she said. The mark of blue on Michael's face stretched spidery legs towards his nose.

"I guess I wouldn't need to experiment on myself if I had a better test subject." He stared at her reflection as his teeth interlocked. Rika's heart dropped. His shoulders trembled as he laughed. "I wouldn't do that to you, would I?" He frowned. "You think I would."

"I think you're capable of anything."

He clucked his tongue.

"I'll take that as a compliment." He gave her a dismissive wave. "I heard Ben was assigned to your case regarding those dead immortals." He breathed on his spectacles and held them to the light. "I didn't think Stone would send a hunter to do it."

"What do you mean?"

"Only an immortal can kill another immortal. Sending a hunter against an immortal is suicide, or murder, however you want to look at it."

"Stone wouldn't dare."

"Wouldn't he?" Michael leaned towards her. "I heard you're pretty close to that hunter." He gave her a pat on the head. She gritted her teeth and stepped back. His lips curled.

"Poor girl." He turned towards the wall he had come from. "By the way, I wouldn't spend so much time staring out the walls. Humans need to do what humans are made to do."

"And what is that?" She felt the heat gather around her neck.

"Follow the rules. It's for your own good." He took a step forward and disappeared through the wall.

· · ·

Rika pressed the button. A mug appeared on the triangular panel. She picked it up and held it close to her mouth. The steam issued the smell of roasted coffee as it rose in frail wisps towards her nose. She sipped the mixture of chemicals and felt a pang of nostalgia for the lost art of instant coffee.

She followed the length of white-washed walls and paused before a black curtain. Drawing it aside, she passed beneath a dim red light that made her skin glow like fire as she crossed into the next room. She placed the mug on the bench and studied a series of photos pinned to the wall.

She smiled at the closest photo of an animal with a long neck. Small ears jutted from its triangular head and its body was covered in large spots. She glanced at the next. A beast of orange fur and black stripes glared at her. Its razor jaws reminded her of Ben.

She picked up her mug and crossed to the furthest wall, pressing her palm upon a screen. The wall made a click and shifted into a doorway. She convulsed in shivers as cold air rushed at her. She hurried in.

Rectangular prisms were slotted into the walls in neat rows. She fumbled at a prism with numb fingers and managed to jerk it from its slot. She looked at the double-helix that floated within.

"Detail," she said and the prism glowed.

"Panthera leo, from family Felidae, more commonly known as, Lion," said a voice from the prism. "Signature is complete and ready for extraction."

"Show me, humans." Rika clamped her jaw to stop the grind of her teeth. A prism above her head shimmered blue. She jerked it from the slot and slammed the door behind her as she returned to her mug. She sculled the contents, waiting for the chemicals to furnace her stomach.

She placed the prism in a slot beside a perspex rod. Blue light spread from the prism and projected a screen, upright, across the table. A double helix rotated in the light. She circled the bench. "Bring up IAP-3. Advise progress."

"Immortal Assimilation Project is seventy per cent complete." Another double helix appeared beside the first.

"Hey, doc!" Ben poked his head through the curtains. "Thought you'd be here."

"A girl has to work," she said. Ben looked at the image rotating above the bench.

"What is it this time? Extracting the strength of a bear to assimilate to my signature?" Ben flexed his biceps.

"No, your last assimilation nearly killed you. I had to rewrite your signature from scratch." She ushered him out of the room. He made a face and lifted the black curtain.

"Ladies first," he said. She smiled, stepping past him.

"So what did you want?"

"Thought you might need this." He dug his hands into his pockets. She looked at the crystal pill he held out to her. Her forehead creased.

"How did you get a pass? Wait, did you —"

Ben's eyes darkened. "No, it's not from a hunt. This comes from Stone. He says you can go outside to finish your research. I'm just following orders."

"From Stone? Why would he —"

"Stop asking questions. Do you want it or not?" He grinned and snatched his hand away as she reached for it. "Not so fast. You have to pay the deliverer first," he said.

"Ben . . . " She placed her hands on her hips.

"What are you thinking?" He gave her a tap on the forehead. Her brain slammed into the back of her skull.

"Ben!" She cupped her head, forcing her feet to stay firm beneath her.

"Sorry, I forgot." He peered into her face. "Are you ok?" Her head throbbed.

"The last time you did that I was in the infirmary for two weeks!"

"Sorry . . . " Ben's tail swished behind him as he tilted his head, looking at the ground. "You've extracted so many signatures for us hunters. I don't understand why you never assimilate yourself."

"Messing with DNA is a sensitive process. Not all humans can survive it. Think of those who died just trying to assimilate to hunter.

I need to find the mix that can make everyone stronger, not just the select few."

"You could survive. If I recall right, you're the only Alpha M left. You could assimilate into an immortal like the others."

"I can't. There's a side effect."

"A side effect?"

"Just look at the immortals. They've forgotten what it means to be human."

"Rika."

"Forget it." She shook her head. "So what payment did you want?"

He studied her face. "I get to come with you."

"You'll get bored."

"Maybe." He shrugged. "I guess I could always leave."

She looked out the window and nodded.

"Okay." She felt as though her bones would snap as Ben gripped her arm.

"Hold still," he said, as she squirmed. She bit her lip. He pressed the crystal pill against her wrist. The pill crumbled into fine dust and seeped into her pores. She shivered as a wave of ice swept up her body. He released her and crossed to the door, pausing. "Rika, do you really believe everyone can survive out there?"

She turned and stared out the window, watching the scattered bricks on the broken street melt like snowflakes in the rain. Heaviness weighed her shoulders. She shrugged it off and nodded.

"We'll head out in the morning."

• • •

Rika stopped before the entryway as rays of green flared between twin arches in a crisscross pattern. The guards turned from the entryway and stared at her from behind the eyeholes of white masks. She glanced behind them. The ruins glowed beneath a dome of red, as a firestorm withdrew into the distance.

LORE

"Sorry, Doctor Grey, you know the rules. Only hunters and immortals can leave Haven without a pass," one of the guards said.

The sound of his muffled voice whistled from the thin slit in his mask.

"It's fine. She's with me."

Rika turned as Ben approached. His leather jacket creaked as he lifted his hand and waved. Rika glanced at his pack. It sat like a turtleshell on his back.

"She'll need clearance, Master Ben."

"She didn't show you?"

She bit back her cry as he twisted her arm to show them the blue mark. The guard's eyes pierced her from behind the mask.

"You're clear, Master Ben," the guard said after a moment. Ben grinned and released her. She rubbed at the bruises on her wrist. He pushed her forward.

The rays drilled fire into her, the blue mark spreading across her body and freezing the sweat on her skin as it formed a protective coating on her flesh.

"Come on," Ben said. She crossed beneath the arches. The stench hit her as if she had walked into a brick wall. Her breath caught and she choked on the fumes that seared through her lungs. She pulled on the mask that hung around her neck. Filtered air flowed through her nose. She adjusted the lens of the mask and turned to Ben. He grinned.

"That smell bothering you?" He drew in a deep breath.

"I'm not a hunter, remember?" She frowned and looked back as guards appeared on the steps above, dashing towards the entryway.

"We better go," Ben said. His pace was fast as he pulled her down the slope.

"Doctor Grey!" shouted a voice from behind. Ben's grip tightened.

"Ben, wait."

Ben's face set and his teeth grit together.

"Don't worry about it. We're almost there," he said.

"Stop them!" Hunters leapt from the glass stairs and charged after them. Ben swore.

"Run!" He began to drag her.

"Ben, why are we —" The scream caught in her throat as blood exploded onto her face. Ben dropped to his knees. It took her a moment to realise he had been shot.

"Rika! Run!" Ben scrambled to his feet. Hot blood stained the floor and the crackle of gunfire rang behind them. Shockwaves shook the air as Ben turned to face the hunters. His tail reared like a cobra behind him, the fur bristling. The air wavered as a pulse from his tail shockwaved the air. The spray of fire-coated bullets froze around them, held in mid-air by an invisible force. His tail whipped the ground. The bullets shot backwards, pelting the hunters like hailstones. Rika felt Ben's grip on the back of her jacket. She ran.

• • •

Rika gasped for breath. The wall crumbled where she pressed it with her palm. She adjusted her mask and coughed. Ben placed his backpack on the floor of ash, his tail sweeping clear the path of footprints they had left.

"We have to keep going. They'll catch us if we stay here," he said.

"Why the hell are we running?" Rika spun and shoved him. She watched in surprise as he fell flat on his back. He groaned, clutching the stain of blood beneath his jacket. She forced aside the urge to run to him.

He climbed to his feet, his tail tightening like a tourniquet around his shoulder as she looked at the backpack on the ground. She crossed to it, yanking it open. Her breath caught. She pulled out the rectangular prism, the other prisms chiming together as they knocked against each other.

Her eyes flicked to Ben.

"Is this why?"

LORE

"Rika . . ." He flinched as she threw the prism at his face.

"Is this why they're shooting at us? You idiot!" Rika leapt forward. Ben's cheeks grew red as she slapped at him. Her tears began to fog her mask. She dropped to her knees as he caught her wrists.

"Rika, look at me." He softened his grip, kneeling to be level with her. "Stone is using your IAP-3 research to create immortals without the human signature as its base."

She stared at him.

"Stone can't be that reckless," she said. "Immortals without any concept of humanity would be uncontrollable. They'd wipe out everything before the firestorms get a chance."

"That's the idea. He wants to create a line of pure immortals." His grip loosened. "The dead immortals were his test subjects. Failed experiments from heart failure. That's why the bodies were showing up without them. Stone was trying to hide what he was doing. I found the last one before he died. He's the one who gave me the pill to get you out. You have to trust me, Rika. I wouldn't lie to you."

Rika stared at his face. Her eyes trailed to the blood on his shirt. She nodded. His expression softened as he expelled a breath. He touched her arm.

"If we can find a place to hole down, you can finish your research; fix the side-effect. Then maybe we'll have a chance."

Rika glanced at the backpack of prisms.

"Even if we manage to hide from the hunters, you know we can't withstand the rain."

"Stone designed these for the hunters." Ben pulled a coat from his pack. "They can fend off the acid."

"What about the firestorms?"

"I thought that was part of your research."

"It's possible through a complete IAP-3 assimilation, but I never got that far." She shook her head, glancing at the clouds and then back at the pyramids. "There's a research facility further south, but they'll guess we'll be heading there. Our only chance is in Haven."

"We can't go back in there!"

"There's an immortal that might be able to help. He'll have the equipment I need to finish my research."

"Can you trust him?"

"No, but you'll bleed to death if we wait. I'll need to assimilate a lizard signature to you."

Ben's forehead furrowed. "A lizard?"

"When a lizard loses its tail, it grows back again," she said.

"I don't need another tail."

"Ben..."

He forced a grin, throwing the backpack over his shoulder. He cringed as the pack brushed against his wound.

"All the entrances to Haven are guarded except the hunters' dorms. It's a hell of a maze to get through though."

"Can we make it?"

"We'll have to." He gritted his teeth and glanced at the black sky. "That storm will be here in an hour."

She nodded as they picked their way through the mountains of ash and rubble.

. . .

They knelt by the wall, shielded by a charred mound of stone. Rika lifted her hand, staring at the ash that coated her fingers. The blue on her skin had shifted to veins that bulged as they stretched outwards, forming a sun-like mark on the top of her hand. Ben knelt beside her, a droplet of sweat trickling down his pale face.

"Stay low. We don't know who's watching from up there."

Rika looked up at the pyramids that stood like mountains around the ruins where they knelt. Ben turned to her, adjusting the hood over her head. She noticed the tremble in his hands, but said nothing as he turned away again. His tail slithered behind him, burying a trickle of blood that dripped from his arm.

The centre of the sun on her hand shifted, losing a fraction.

"The pill's starting to wear off," she said.

"How long?"

She showed him the mark. He nodded.

"We can make for the underground. There's a way into the dorms from there." They hugged the walls through the ruins, the ash clinging to them, adding to the camouflage of their coats.

Rika breathed deep through her mask, the goggles fogging up around the edges. She moved close to Ben, noting his pace had slowed.

"Let me have a look at that wound," she said.

"I'm fine. We're almost there."

They circled a shattered tower, the steeple weathered and smote by fire. Ben shoved her onto her back. She wheezed, struggling for breath as he smothered her mask, pressing her head into the black earth. She struggled, hitting at him.

"Hold still!" His voice was a hiss in her ears. She clawed at him, feeling her body weaken. Black spots appeared on her vision.

She tugged at his hand. His grip loosened and she gulped air as it began to flow again through her mask.

"Keep searching. They couldn't be far," said a voice. She froze, listening to the flurry of footsteps. They passed, fading into the distance.

"Were you trying to kill me?" She looked at Ben, but he was still. "Ben . . . " She rose, shaking him. He failed to stir. "Ben!"

She gripped his shoulders. He drew in a sharp breath, his eyes opening wide.

"Rika, stop!" His face screwed up and he brushed her hand from the wound she was clutching at.

"I'm sorry, I thought . . . " She looked at his blood on her hand.

"I wouldn't do that to you." He took it, wiping the blood onto his sleeve. "Come on, they're gone now."

They followed the length of the wall, ducking at the openings that formed windows in a collapsed building. They descended a slope into the basement, crawling over broken stairs until they reached a series of tunnels that glowed red and stunk of sulphur.

"How long?" Ben said. She looked at the mark on her hand.

"Three quarters."

"Then we have ten minutes before the firestorm hits." His pace quickened and she pulled at the collar of her coat, the sweat making her skin itch. She broke into a run, puffs of hot air beating at her from behind. She glanced at the holes overhead as thin buttons of flame illuminated their path.

"I think the firestorm's going to hit sooner than ten minutes," she said.

Ben grunted, a trail of blood forming a path for her. She rushed forward as he collapsed.

"We're almost there." He gagged a winded breath. "Just need to make it through."

She took the backpack from him and froze, staring at the blood that seeped through his coat.

"Come on," she said. She slid his arm over her shoulder, helping him stand. His feet dragged and she forced him forward, struggling with his weight. They inched down a tunnel and rounded a bend where a glass wall barred their path. Several doors dotted the surface, each woven together by a different element.

"Which door do you want? Fire or water?"

Ben grunted and shook his head.

"Those are decoys. We need —" He pushed her back. "Watch out!"

She felt the shockwaves pass through his body and he crumbled. She turned and felt the sting of a bullet against her cheek. Her skull trembled and her vision blurred as her face struck the gravel. She heard a shout and glimpsed the sleeve of a leather coat.

"Mic . . . " The next blow jolted her brain into darkness.

· · ·

The ring in her ears made her stomach turn. Rika tried to move but her body was paralysed. She opened an eye, but the glare forced it shut again.

"IAP-3, stage four, complete. Assimilation of all recorded Felidae family signatures . . . successful," said a computerised voice.

Rika felt a hand scratch under her chin. A strange sense of pleasure ran up her body.

"You will bear the feline grace well, just like your mother . . . God rest her soul," said a voice that hovered above her face. She heard the snap of fingers close to her ear. It made her head twist upon itself. She tried to cover her ears, but her hands refused to respond.

"Subject shows high sensitivity to sound. Two hundred per cent more than calculated."

"Just what I expected from an Alpha M. Begin stage five."

"She'll never forgive you for this, Michael."

Rika recognised the voice. She tried to place a face to it and failed.

"There's a lot of things she'll never forgive me for, but this is the only way she'll live. You want her to live, don't you?"

Rika felt the touch on her hand.

"Not like this."

"We have no choice. Stone is close to completing his own tests. No hunter will be able to withstand his immortals. He'll have created more than he can handle."

"And Rika?"

"We won't be able to handle her either, but Ben, there's nothing else I can do. If she dies, so does her research."

"Is that all you care about?"

"That's not what I meant. I would never use her."

"Then what are you doing now?"

"Stage five complete. Beginning stage six."

Rika felt the strength flow through her veins.

"Rika." The voice was like a breath of air. She could smell the mixture of mint and a touch of coffee on each spoken word.

"I'm sorry . . . for everything."

Rika heard the sound. It was a faint flutter like the wing of a butterfly. It grew at a gradual pace until it rumbled like distant thunder.

"Ben."

"Rika, I'm here."

She felt the touch on her hand. "Ben, they're coming."

The hand snatched away. She heard the scuffle of footsteps beneath the roar.

"Michael, it's Stone. They're crossing the lower levels."

"We can't move her yet!"

"I'll try to lure them off."

"Ben . . . " Rika breathed a sigh.

"Stage six, complete."

• • •

The double-helix floated in the darkness. Rika poked at the signature, forcing the double-helix to mutate and multiply. She looked at Michael as he leaned close and examined the image. He smiled at her, patting her on the head.

"Do you see?" he said. "Somewhere in there, you learn to tell the difference between right and wrong."

"Isn't that the same place that brings so much hurt?"

"Yes, but without it, you are just another animal."

"Sometimes animals act more human than we do."

"A sad truth, but this fundamental unit is what makes us human. Animals abandon their weak, but in humans, the duty of the strong is to protect the weak."

"Protect them?"

A silhouette formed against the light behind them.

"Dinner's ready, dear."

Rika recognised her mother's voice. She looked back at the silhouette, but saw only the light illuminating the figure.

LORE

"We'll be right in," he said. He smiled and took Rika's hand.

"Come on, let's go before mummy gets angry."

Rika opened her eyes and blinked away the glare. Her pupils drew away from the speck on the ceiling, refocusing on the face that hovered over her. Michael lifted his spectacles.

"How do you feel?" he said. She inched up and looked at the shackles that bound her feet to titanium bars.

"My head hurts," she said. She touched the earmuffs that covered her ears.

"Keep them on. They'll muffle the sound until you adjust," he said. She looked at her hands. There appeared to be no change.

"Where are we?"

"You don't remember? You used to play here when you were little."

Rika glanced around, drawing in the familiar smell of chemicals puffing from tubes along the ceiling. By the window sat a platform where a double-helix was projected. She squinted at it, remembering the silhouette of her mother standing behind it.

"How did we get here?" she said.

"You were attacked by hunters. I brought you in."

"You?" She scrutinised his face, but his expression was impenetrable. She glanced behind him.

"Where's Ben?"

Michael removed his spectacles and placed them on a metal tray beside several tubes.

"They've taken him."

"They?"

"Stone."

Rika gaped at Michael. His mouth remained shut, yet she could hear his circle of thoughts. She blinked and her mind flitted through his skull, drilling through his synapses.

Her mind jolted from his, as images of armed hunters flooded into her thoughts from outside. She clutched at her head and screamed. The tinted glass shattered around them, a chain of explosions making her ears sear. She clenched the earmuffs, blinking flares of light from the front of her vision.

"Rika!" Michael's shout was a whisper compared to the rumble of thoughts in her head. She blinked and her vision cleared enough for her to see the hunters dangling outside the shattered walls. Fire-coated bullets exploded from their guns.

Michael stepped before her and slid his spectacles in place. She heard a light chime from the movement and the flames around the bullets dissipated mid-air, their empty shells striking the ground.

"Do you know why hunters never duel with immortals?" Michael straightened his spectacles. "Immortals are smarter."

Rika heard the chime again and the shards on the ground shot up, slicing the ropes. The hunters screamed as they dropped.

"They're also over-confident."

Rika turned, hearing the snap of bone. She looked at Michael who dangled in the air. Stone twisted the knife, wedging it into Michael's spine. Michael slid to the floor, his face turning a tinge of blue as his legs began to solidify.

"Did you think only doctors could invent things?" Stone said as he jerked out the knife, examining the serrated edge. "I call this Soul Reaper or SR15, if you like." Stone swiped the knife.

Rika blinked. The knife sliced silver lines in the air. She tilted her head, fixated, as the lines faded again.

"Why fifteen?" she said. Stone looked at her in surprise. She looked at Michael who had solidified into a block of ice. "Did one to fourteen fail?"

Stone's nostrils flared. He rushed forward, stabbing the knife into her stomach. She blinked. He released her, stumbling back with the knife in his hand. The blade was bent sideways as if it would snap. She heard the beep and the shackles around her legs unlocked as a voice blared from the speakers.

"IAP-3, final stage complete. Assimilation of all recorded signatures . . . successful." Rika tried to stand. She sprang to her feet instead and landed an inch from Stone. Her vision multiplied before they focused on his icy face. The shock faded from his eyes. He smiled.

"I see you've completed your tests, but like I said, Ms. Rika, not only doctors invent things."

She sensed the heat drop from above. She leapt back, the air whipping like a typhoon behind her as she swept through it, landing beside the shattered walls.

The creature darted from the ceiling to the floor, its speed making it look like a shadow as it flashed beside Stone, landing in a crouch. Its leather jacket materialised over a pair of jeans, a long tail rising over the bowed head.

"I call him H700," Stone said.

"Six hundred and ninety-nine fails," Rika said. Stone's eyes darkened. The creature beside Stone lifted its head and snarled a set of jagged teeth. Memories flooded her head and she drew back.

"Ben . . ."

The eyes snapped onto her face. The fur bristled and Ben's fingers shaped into claws, shattering the tiles beneath his hands.

"My first successful heartless. I now have the ability to iron out the weaknesses that brought us to our current state. Only the strong are worthy to live," Stone said. A torrent of thoughts spun in her head, gripping a part of her core. She sifted them.

"Strength is given to protect . . . not destroy."

"You see, Doctor Grey, that is what makes you weak." He patted Ben on the head. "Kill her."

Ben lunged at her with the force of an explosion. She sidestepped and he shot out of the broken walls. His tail whipped behind him, the slither of fur wrapping around her wrist and dragging her towards the opening.

She growled and dug her feet into the ground, pulling the tail taut. Ben jerked mid-air. His tail bristled. Spikes jabbed from it, splitting her palm. She ripped her hand free, blood squirting from the gashes. Ben landed on a mound of rubble, turning back and snarling up at her. She brushed the blood away, staring at the wound as it knit itself together.

She jumped, smelling the sweat on the rush of air. The ground shattered, erupting beneath her. Ben burst through behind her, gripping her by the hair and jerking her to him. He crushed her in a body slam, propelling them through the hole. They crashed through several levels of cement, falling to the bottom of the pyramid.

Rika screamed as her eardrums burst, unable to filter the roar of sound bashing at her. She blinked at the earmuffs that lay in a twisted heap beside her as she clutched at her ears. Ben stood over her. He jerked her head back, driving his knee into her spine until it snapped. She fell limp. He threw her.

She crashed through the glass wall, sprawling onto the mound of rubble. She breathed ash as she looked at the ruined buildings, then at the black sky overhead. Streaks of lightning twisted around the smog, but no sound reached her ears. The first drop of rain touched her skin. It devoured her flesh.

The shadow fell over her. She blinked at Ben as his tail lashed behind him, the rain searing holes through his shirt. She looked at the familiar face as the dull throb in her ears began to lift and her ability to hear returned in a series of slow clicks. She could smell the sweat of the hunters beneath their heavy rainproof clothes as they circled her.

"Finish her off." Stone's voice sounded like the scratch of metal on glass. She felt her spine realign and movement returned to her fingers. Her lips drew into a smile as her skin reconstructed itself, sieving drops of acid from her pores. Something flickered in Ben's gaze as he watched her. His jagged teeth set in a grin.

"A lizard," he said. Stone's footsteps paused above her head.

"What are you waiting for?" he said.

"There's no point." Ben turned to him. She lifted her gaze and glimpsed the firestorm brewing overhead.

"It grows back. Just like a tail."

"I don't care if she grows wings! Kill her!" Stone stepped forward and struck Ben across the head. Ben blinked, as if a fly had landed near his eye. He rubbed at the stubble that had sprouted from his chin, then sent Stone flying into a row of hunters with a kick. He squatted beside Rika. The black sky turned to flares of light.

"Kill them! Kill them both!"

The hunters rushed towards them. Rika saw the flash above.

"Ben!" He dove onto her as columns of fire rained from the clouds. She clamped her eyes shut as their surroundings turned to flame.

. . .

"Trial conversion complete," said the voice from the speaker.

"Detail."

"Subject shows the ability to self-purify air through the lungs. Survival rate outside Haven increased by one hundred per cent."

The window shattered as the figure crashed through the clear glass and landed in a crouch.

"Ben, I just had that fixed. Maybe you should practice with the door?"

Ben glanced at the door. It exploded into pieces.

"Ben!"

"Sorry, Michael."

"You would have made the perfect heartless. You're lucky your signature was incompatible thanks to Rika's rewrite, otherwise that pile of ash out there would be her and not Stone and his lackeys."

"Rika." Ben turned and looked out the window. "Where is she?"

Michael adjusted his spectacles. "Where else?"

Ben's jagged teeth drew into a grin. He leapt from the window and landed on the patch of grass. He looked down the ash-coated road where the occasional flower bloomed, scattering its perfumed scent into the smog-filled air. His eyes lifted to the lone field, the only section of cleared rubble covered in patches of grass. His pupils retracted as they focused on the herd of long-necked creatures, covered in brown spots, that ran through the field alongside a lone figure. A single ray of sunlight pierced the black sky, shedding light over her.

"Rika," he said with a smile. He bolted.

BENEATH THE LOVELIEST TINTS OF AZURE
Jeff Samson

"You sure picked a hell of a day to start."

The guard stared up at Ted with a look somewhere between aggravation and indifference. He slouched over his desk, his belly spilling over a portion of its tidy surface. His chair creaked in protest as he swiveled lazily.

"I'm sorry?" Ted said, deepening his voice to match the guard's husky bass.

The guard wiped a hand over his head, polished bald but for a faint horseshoe of salt and pepper hair buzzed to the same length as the patchy stubble on his face. He pushed himself away from his desk, growling as he rose.

"Ken Allen," he said, enveloping Ted's comparably slight hand in a powerful grip.

"Ted Kirsch." Ted stifled an urge to wince.

"I know — Hurrel's replacement. Been expecting you." Ken pursed his lips. "Sorry if I seem a bit gruff. It's just, well, visiting days aren't exactly best for breaking in fresh meat. Know what I mean?"

Ted nodded that he did. Then quickly realized that he didn't.

"Visiting days?" he asked. "Here? I didn't think they let anyone in from the outside."

Ken rubbed his temples and sighed.

"It's a strictly inside thing," he said. "An inter-inmate thing. They each get one visiting day a year on the anniversary of their incarceration. Warden says it reminds our guests why they're here — keeps guilt high and hope low. Know what I mean?"

Again Ted nodded, but he still didn't understand. He was about to ask more questions, when Ken's face hardened.

"What's that?" Ken barked, pointing to Ted's chest.

Ted looked down, expecting to find something that shouldn't be there. But all seemed as it should.

"What's what?"

"Good God, man, is that a pen?" Ken shouted.

Ted looked down at the ballpoint pen in his chest pocket.

"Um . . . yes."

Ken reached out and withdrew it from Ted's uniform. He snapped it in half and tossed it in the aluminum garbage can beside his desk where it landed with a clatter.

"Are you nuts, man?" he asked. "Do you have any idea what kind of damage a pen could cause down here — the things the people we guard could conjure up if they got hold of it? Weren't you briefed about this place?"

Ted felt mildly annoyed that Ken presumed a fellow guard — or anyone, for that matter — would need to be briefed on Hydro Facility 237. The prison was as legendary outside the system as it was within.

And Ted had always had a special fascination with the place. He'd read articles and books about everything from its engineering to its inmates. He'd sought out old screws, who traded second-hand tall tales for pints. He was intrigued that the deeper he dug, the blurrier the lines between fact and fiction became. It seemed the only certainty he found was that no one on the inside ever called Hydro Facility 237 by its official name. To the warders who had paced the damp cavernous hall for more than two centuries, the prison was simply The Grotto.

Ted raised his hands as if to fend off Ken's invective. *Whoa*, Ted thought. *Does this guy really expect me to know every rule and regulation by heart on the first day? It's a pen, for Christ's —*

The shock of realization shattered the thought in his head.

Oh Ted. He felt his face slacken. *You stupid, stupid man.* He lowered his hands, burning with embarrassment, stunned that he could be so careless.

With some difficulty, Ken rounded his desk and lumbered towards the young guard. He brought his nose to within a few inches of Ted's.

"Now you listen here, rookie," he snarled. "There's just two rules you need to remember around here. No writing implements of any kind. And always stay extra alert on visiting days. Don't take your eyes off either one of them for a second, you hear?"

Ted nodded, genuinely this time.

"Good."

A buzzer blared and a large red light pulsed above the entrance to the guardroom.

Ken flashed Ted a wry smile.

"Well, how 'bout that?" he said. "Perfect timing."

•   •   •

The frail old man entered through the heavy, tarnished brass door, flanked by two hulking guards, each clasping a thin, sinewy arm. His hands and feet were manacled with bulky brass cuffs chained together with links as thick as fingers. A third, even thicker chain joined the two sets of restraints, greatly hindering the prisoner's movement. As his escorts stepped into the room, he shuffled forward inch by inch. His ancient shoes brushed the polished concrete floor in quick, quiet sighs.

His face was gaunt and deeply lined, its paper-thin skin sagging lifelessly over bare bone. His eyes were the soft, even grey of overcast skies — a mere tinge of pale green rimmed his smoky pupils. The few wisps of ghostly hair sprouting from his liver-spotted head looked petrified in place like tenuous fossils.

The guard at the old man's left extended a small leather binder to Ken.

"Oh yes," Ken said. He took the binder and turned to Ted. "Standard sign-off procedure," he said evenly.

Ken thumbed through a stack of yellowed pages filled with hand-stamped entries. When he came to a page with an empty row, he reached for the stamp on his desk. He rolled the correct rubber numbers into place, and hammered it into the empty box, leaving an indentation of his signature, the date, and the time in their appropriate columns, just beneath the inmate's identification number.

The guard slipped the binder from Ken's hands and slammed it shut.

"He's all yours," he said.

As Ken and Ted each grasped an arm, the escorting guards backed out of the room. Again the buzzer sounded and the light flared. The heavy door thudded shut.

· · ·

"All right, Herman," Ken said to the old man. "Let's take it slow."

They walked the old man to the opposite end of the guardroom, stopping before another large, metal door. Ken reached for his side and unclasped the keys from his belt. Ted had never seen this configuration before — four keys threaded side-by-side through a cylinder of brass. It looked like fingers on a hand.

LORE

Ted saw Ken insert each key into its corresponding hole and turn, which produced small metallic clicks. As he turned the final key, hidden mechanisms within the door came to life. Gears creaked and moaned. Tumblers ratcheted and thunked into line. Cylinders scraped through shafts and thudded out of their locked position. As Ted watched, wide-eyed, the door eased open with a feeble whine.

Cold, clammy air flooded the room, redolent with salt, mildew and fish.

Ted lowered his head and tried to bury his nose in his shoulder to stifle a gag.

"Ah, yes," said Ken, "I should have warned you about the smell."

Ted shook his head, exhaling hard. As he breathed in, he was surprised to find the musty air tinged with the metallic tang of ink and heavy stench of moldy books.

"Yeah . . . that's certainly . . . certainly a hell of a stink."

"You'll get used to it."

"I doubt that."

"So do I." Ken smirked. "OK, let's give the man his hour's worth."

Ken reached for an electrical box alongside the door and raised the lever with a flick of his wrist. A warm, buttery light seeped into the guardroom from the space beyond.

Following Ken's lead, Ted slowly stepped into the vast room with the old man in tow.

· · ·

Ted gasped as he entered the chamber. While only fifty feet wide, it was several hundred yards long and at least two hundred feet high. The soaring metal walls were all but entirely marbled with a bronze, blood and soot-black patina. Only a few unmarred stretches of burnished gold caught the chamber's meager light to reveal the solid brass beneath. Set within those walls, like portals in the hull of some unfathomably large submarine, were hundred-foot-wide panes of glass, rimmed in smooth, bulbous rivets that bled verdigris from their seams.

Every inch of metal was slick with condensation. Rivulets of tarnished water traced ragged paths of corrosion and grime and trickled into the slimy gutters that lined the corridor. Against the ceaseless thrum and groan of machinery unseen, the cavernous space resounded with the patter, gurgle and slurp of water finding its way home.

"My God." Ted's jaw hung open.

"Yeah, it's something," Ken said, his smile proud.

"I mean... I'd read... I'd heard... but..."

"There's roughly 20 million cubic feet of seawater in each cell." Ken's tone ranged between teacherly and boastful. "And the walls extend another fifty feet above the waves. Oxygen is pumped in from the surface, water is filtered from the surrounding ocean." Ken paused and gazed down the length of the chamber. "It's a hell of a facility."

Ted shook his head, eyes wide.

"Well then," Ken said, "I think you can manage from here."

Ted shot a look at Ken in disbelief. "What? What do you mean?"

"Young man, it's quite a walk to get to where he needs to go. My knees aren't what they used to be. Besides, you came highly recommended — I'm sure you can handle it."

Ted felt his mouth go dry.

"Yeah, but... don't I... I mean... isn't there a training period or something?"

Ken laughed.

"Oh, I'm afraid it's sink or swim around here, kid." He motioned down the corridor. "There — I had McGowan from the night shift set up a chair."

Ted looked about two hundred yards down the corridor, barely able to see the small metal chair in the low, wavering light.

"Uh... all... right," Ted stammered.

Ken slapped him on the shoulder.

"Relax. It's a cake walk. Just remember what I said about keeping your eyes peeled." He gave the old man a head to toe. "Though I don't think you have much to worry about with this old-timer."

"What?" Ted blurted. "Keep my eyes peeled? Please tell me I don't have to stand there with him while he's —"

"It's only for an hour. And I'll be right here. Just holler if you need me." Ken turned to step back into the guardroom, but stopped himself mid-stride. He turned back to Ted. "Oh, and I'd keep my eyes forward if I were you." His mouth smiled, but his eyes did not. "Some awful stuff here in our little aquarium."

Ted watched him walk away. He sighed and turned to the old man in his custody, who was hanging silent and expressionless in his hands.

"Guess it's just you and me," Ted said.

• • •

The two moved forward at a painfully slow pace, Ted taking small, halting steps, the old man shuffling along.

As they neared the first portal, Ted recalled Ken's advice. But not even the strongest of wills could have ignored the overwhelming presence looming on the other side of the glass.

Ted craned his head up and to his left. Six massive snake-like heads stared back at him. Each rested at the end of a long, serpentine neck that wound away towards a body rendered a dark and blurry outline by the murky water. Each pair of tortoise-sized eyes seemed to follow him with unflinching bitterness and disdain. Three heads opened their wicked maws, baring three concentric rows of fat, translucent teeth as tall as the men they had long ago ripped from the deck of Ulysses' home-bound vessel. Their companions flitted forked purple tongues over horned, scaly jaws.

Ted looked at the edge of the portal and was relieved to find that the walls and glass were at least ten feet thick. He followed the arc of rivets down to a grimy plaque bolted in place beneath the rim. It read H-800-B in thick, embossed characters.

He gazed down the hall. But something drew his attention to the portal on his right.

The water in the cell marked HH-1824 was only a few feet deep. A dozen yards from the portal, a large granite rock rose from the placid surface, dominating the interior. Ted's eyes widened as he followed the rock's upward slope to the vision perched on its stony summit.

Her skin was alabaster, her flaxen hair flowing around her shoulders and down her back, pooling about her like a blanket of gold. She combed her hair slowly, methodically, drawing a fine-toothed abalone comb down and out, down and out, through the same strands of shining hair. She paused, turned and locked her gaze on his.

Below her sad blue eyes, her mouth was firmly gagged with a balled-up crimson ribbon, silencing the golden voice that had for centuries lured love-struck mariners to dash their ships into kindling upon their rocky pedestals. Frayed strands spilled from between her deeply fissured lips like strips of bloody meat.

Ted turned away quickly and moved on with his charge.

Slowly, all but soundlessly, they made their way past a giant, coral-colored squid resting languidly at the bottom of cell JV-1870, its jet black eyes not registering their presence, its many tentacles slowly rising and falling about the eroded wreck of the Nautilus like loops of strange, underwater foliage. Then past a massive Great White, twenty-five feet from nose to tail — the scourge of Amity Island and one of the prison's two most recent additions — who paused from chomping on a rusted-out dive tank to swim back and forth along the portal, knocking its scarred snout against the glass of PB-1974.

As Ted turned to the still distant chair, he felt a wave of anger wash over him. It was as if the portals had opened, allowing The Grotto's fetid waters to rush into the great, yawning chamber, flooding Ted's thoughts with the oceans of blood these creatures had spilled. His mind coursed with currents reddened by the scores of sailors, soldiers and swimmers they'd drowned, gnashed and swallowed, all at the whim of the men who'd summoned them forth. It sank into the lightless deep to dwell in the necropolis of their making, where fractured hulls slumped like mausoleums and upturned rudders marked unnamed graves. It overflowed with the tears of flesh and blood families and friends left broken and mourning.

His eyes darting between the vile things that flanked his path, wasting away in their putrid cells, he was overcome with a sense of purpose — a righteousness that set his gut aflame and crackled electric over his skin. *They deserve this endless incarceration*, he thought. And turning to his prisoner, feeling his face flush and draw taut with contempt, he was certain the old man deserved it, too.

. . .

At last they came to the portal with the small chair before it. HM-1851, read the plaque beneath the glass — same as the ragged label on the old man's chest.

"Sit down," Ted hissed, still in the grip of fury.

The old man said nothing. He merely stared at the cloudy water in what appeared to Ted to be an empty cell.

"I said sit down."

Again the old man said nothing. And Ted was nearly too slow placing the chair underneath him as he started to sit without warning.

"All right, old man," Ted said, "your hour starts —"

Something in Ted's periphery drew his attention. He turned to the tank, and caught sight of a shape beginning to define itself far back in the filthy water — a soft, subtle lightening of space. It brightened as it neared the portal, its fuzzy, slightly oval form sharpening. And after a few short moments, Ted found himself face to face with an unnaturally large, uncannily colored whale.

The creature pressed its snow-white forehead against the glass, its flesh so thoroughly slashed, cleaved and pocked it appeared to be etched with ancient runes. As it swayed slowly from side to side, it revealed a brown and white-flecked body bristling with the splintered shafts of harpoons, and enmeshed in a latticework of nets, ropes and rigging. Lashed tight against the beast's side was a gnawed, barnacle-encrusted skeleton — its arms splayed wide, its neck bound in a coil of blackened rope. The jagged tip of its right femur stirred within the rotting mouth of a wood and leather harness, sprouting a carved ivory peg.

The old man inhaled deeply, then held his breath. He raised his hands to his face. His body shook as he began to whimper.

"Oh . . . oh my boy . . . my boy."

Ted stared in silence as the old man's sobbing grew more intense. He watched his tears flow down his pallid cheeks and splash into his hands.

"I'm so sorry, my boy," he said, wiping spittle from his chin. "I'm so sorry."

Ted didn't understand what the old man was apologizing for. But that didn't matter. It was clear he felt a deep remorse for the murderous creature's captivity.

"He's killed hundreds," Ted said through clenched teeth. "Even thousands by some accounts." He felt his throat tighten. "He deserved to be hunted down and thrown in —"

The old man withdrew his face from his hands.

"Hunted down? Is that the story they tell?"

The old man shook his head and laughed — the sound brittle, defeated. He turned slowly to meet Ted's gaze. His pale eyes flared as he spoke.

"*I* put him in here," he snarled. "The bastards put a pen in my hand and a gun in my mouth and said give us the whale. And I . . . I was too craven to defy them . . . I put my own life before his."

The old man's words enveloped Ted in a disquieting chill, turning his skin to goose-flesh. He stood, listening, the hair on the back of his neck rising.

"I may well deserve this," the prisoner said, just above a whisper. "But he . . ."

LORE

As if responding to the old man's lament, the whale opened its long, narrow mouth. A stream of thundering, throbbing clicks filled the hall, rattling the portals in their frames.

The old man's jaw went slack. He leaned forward, pressed his face to the glass, and howled. He brought his hands alongside his sunken, tear-slicked cheeks. His breath plumed from his nose and mouth, forming a fine mist on the cool glass. His long, yellowed nails rapped a quiet rhythm as he gently ran his fingers down the smooth surface, as if stroking the beast's ruined brow.

As Ted watched the old man, the tide of anger that had coursed hotly through him ebbed, leaving in its wake an icy sadness. The tension in him drained. And all he felt was a profound and utter emptiness.

He thought of the old man being dragged down the corridor and dropped in his throne of penance and pain, every year for the last hundred and twenty. He imagined the stark scene playing out long after he himself had walked his final round. Envisioned the endless succession of warders to come, wheeling out the old man's slow-withering form, his gnarled legs dangling feebly, his head propped upright, his heavy eyes pried and fixed open by some grotesque contraption. And for the briefest of moments, Ted felt as though he might join the old man in tears.

Ted found his thoughts drifting to Ken's words. "Don't take your eyes off either of them," he had said. "Not for a second." But seeing the old man's regret twist his decrepit form into a thing even more piteous and meek, he felt the only human thing to do was look away.

He turned his head and gazed down the corridor, allowing the old man a private moment with his creation.

After a few moments, he turned back and stepped to the old man, who looked like he was about to collapse in his chair.

"Sir, please," Ted said, placing his hands on his shoulders and easing him back from the glass, "Let me help . . ."

His words petered out as he caught sight of the glass. Where the old man's hands and face had been, a frosting of breath was fading fast . . . but not fast enough.

Beneath the Loveliest Tints of Azure

Before Ted could react, the letters scratched into the waning cloud leaped from their glassy page, and in a process primal, rote, indescribable, burst into his mind, forming words, phrases, sentences... meaning.

Suddenly, the white whale ceased its cries, whirled around and disappeared into the shadowy depths of its tank. There was a breath of silence, a low, rhythmic thrumming that sent a shiver through metal and glass, loosening the cell floor in roiling clouds of mud, sand and silt. Then the distant sound of waves crashing. And the ear-splitting, klaxon wail of an alarm.

. . .

"What the hell!" screamed Ken.

Ted turned to see the veteran guard barreling towards him, rolls of fat writhing beneath his uniform, legs looking as though they might snap under his weight at any moment.

He stopped a few feet in front of the two men and sunk forward, wincing as he rested his hands on his knees. He wheezed as he spoke, gasping for air between words.

"What happened? What the hell happened?"

Ted didn't speak. He looked down at the old man hanging limp in his arms, his body a parched, gossamer husk, its weight almost imperceptible. The barest trace of a smile still lingered on his breathless lips. Then he turned to the patch of rime on the glass.

Ken followed his stare and found the passage, all but lost with the fleeting mist.

"My God," he said, as he too read.

The white whale threshed its powerful tail, exploded from the shadowy depths of its cell toward the sun-tipped waves, and sailed over the high brass walls into the boundless blue beyond.

ROBOT TIME MACHINES AND THE FEAR OF BEING ALONE
Rebecca M. Latimer

SOMETIMES I WAKE WITH A JOLT in the middle of the night and I'm in a ghost world. The apartment building is empty, the city is silent. The vertical blinds over the windows cast bluish prison bars of shadow over the abundance of *things* in this place, things inanimate, inorganic, and soulless. I can't sleep, so I sit staring through the balcony doors at the dim and lonely city all around me, waiting patiently for the moon to arc across the sky, though it never seems to move.

• • •

A few months ago I found a robot half buried at the edge of a creek near my apartment building. The glint of the evening sun bounced off its body and illuminated sightless light bulb eyes. It was little, with surfaces textured by an orange rust rash, and after using a stick to dig it free I discovered a short black cord dangling in a half-curl from its back. It made me think of old sci-fi posters depicting an imagined future, and I took it for an abandoned toy predicting just the same. Whimsical robot. Riki would have told me to leave it, if she'd known. Her voice entered my head, uninvited: *worthless trash*. I ignored her odd intrusion and stowed the robot in my backpack.

Back at my apartment I deposited my find in the bathtub. I washed it free of the earth's residue, scrubbed it with rust remover, and carefully towelled it dry. I propped it against the living room wall and sort of liked the way it looked there, small and slumped with its cord curled dejectedly around disc-like feet. But of course it had to have some purpose beyond standing in for art, for what we thought the future might be. I plugged its prongs into the wall socket and waited. Its light-bulb eyes began to blink pale orange. *Cool*, I thought, though I'd hoped for more.

I left it and went to bed, and all night those lights were violent. The blinking glow crept under my bedroom door and broke my sleep. When I did sleep I dreamed of my desk, the power button on my computer, the lukewarm coffee and the office chair with the squeaking wheels and of typing, typing, typing. Awake I thought of the rain and the river and I hated everything in the world. I woke again and again until, at some point in the night, I staggered into the living room, fumbled through the darkness, and yanked the robot's cord from the wall. I fell back into bed, hardly remembering the act.

In the morning I found the robot circling my cluttered coffee table like a disoriented puppy, filling the air with the mournful whirring of its feet and dragging that black cord behind it like a tail. I knelt on the floor and watched, amazed, unblinking. "Hello," I said. The robot expressed an ambiguous electrical-sounding response and continued making crop circles in the rug, snagging here and there before breaking free with a frustrated burst of effort from whatever motor it contained. From time to time it stopped to face me, eyes aglow. I laughed.

Monday morning my boss leaned his heavy shoulder against the half-wall surrounding my desk, poisoning the atmosphere of my cu-

LORE

bicle with his snack-food crunching presence. "Hey Sparky," he said. "Hot as a middle-aged stripper outside, am I right? What I wouldn't do for a cool-off." His breath wheezed out of him like a laugh. The foil baggie of flavoured peanuts crinkled in his hand as he dug his fingers inside. "You want some *arachides*?"

"I'm allergic," I muttered, yanking my phone off its base and punching random digits. My boss just stood there as my cheek started sweating under the pressure of the plastic receiver and the voice droned in my ear that this number was not in service. I remembered, out of nowhere, the all-too familiar sound of Riki's answering machine picking up, that giggled *you've reached . . . you know who! And I'm totally sorry I missed you.* Riki always used to screen her calls.

Finally my boss sauntered away, leaving me alone again in my space. I hung up the phone and sat hunched in my chair, thinking of that photograph of Riki I kept hidden, face-down, in my drawer. The last time I'd seen her was, maybe, during the week I took care of my mother's old dog. Riki came over and sprawled like a tiger skin rug across the couch, flat and flimsy with her feet flopped gracelessly on the floor. She cranked the volume on the television set like a teenager, and I remember thinking the mutt was a better conversationalist than she was. I played tug-of-war with him until Riki looked at me and said, "It's only a stupid dog."

I gave her a puzzled frown. "What?"

"Just don't look so pleased with yourself." She looked at the ceiling. "As if you've made a friend."

I imagined, as I came through my apartment door that Monday evening with armfuls of junk mail and takeout, and the robot whirring towards me in greeting, what she would think of this new companion. *There's no soul in there*, she'd insist as the thing whirred over her toes. Practical Riki. The robot followed me through the apartment and settled by my legs in the living room — just like my mother's old dog had — while I dined on grease and cardboard tasting things. The sky trapped outside the balcony doors was already dim and colourless.

Robot Time Machines and the Fear of Being Alone

It had been months since the last time I'd spoken to Riki, I realized, months and months transitioning into years since that final phone call.

At night, with the robot seated humming at my bedside, my eyes would fall shut, and moments later I would jolt awake to an empty room, an empty building, an empty city. I'd go out onto the balcony, taste the strangely chemical air and watch the moon trapped in place across the street. Sometimes my fingertips were silver and black with the blood of machines, my eyes burning like embers in my skull because I'd forgotten how to blink. And Riki felt so strangely far away, part of another life, a story, as if she'd never existed. I thought of her laugh and the blanket fort she made in the woods and her hand on my face the time she caressed and the time she slapped and none of that was real — only the blinking lights, the buzzing, the click-click-click was real.

These were bad dreams.

A daily routine blossomed. I kept the robot's feet and light-bulb eyes clean and made sure it always had a charge. The murmur, buzz, and crackle of its presence became a pleasant white noise crucial to my contentment. I greeted it when I came home from work, wished it sweet dreams before bed. Some might call this taking things too far.

One day the dishwasher leaked sudsy water across the floor of the kitchenette and instead of dealing with it I just stood there, feet soaked, remembering Riki, because our families used to spend summers together at a lakeside cabin owned by somebody's relative. Riki wasn't much older than I was but she seemed it, an ancient and immortal goddess of the water who liked to laugh a lot and sneak cigarettes from her mother's purse. Those were days of golden sunlight shimmering on water droplets and Riki's hands under my arms as she lifted me up and tossed me into the deep. She had a cousin who liked to stand in the shallows, cringing at the cold and running her fingers through her hair like she couldn't help it.

"Can we do something else?" the girl kept saying. "This is stupid."

Riki insisted we were having fun and continued to play with me. She pretended to be a shark, a mermaid, and then made me tread water until my arms and legs burned and I'd swallowed several mouthfuls of the lake. Half in defiance and half wanting to make her laugh some more, I started to thrash and splash, playing sea-monster. Riki squealed and turned away. She threw her arms up over her head. She shouted for me to stop. I leaped on her back and wrapped my arms around her neck, but her foot slipped and we both went crashing down. I sucked back a lungful of water. Riki lurched away and I couldn't hold onto her. For an instant I thought, *I'm alone, and I'm drowning*, and then my head broke the surface. Coughing and terrified, I continued to splash even after I'd found my footing again. Riki was wading up onto the beach, sobbing with her hand clamped over one earlobe. Her cousin ran to her.

"Oh my gosh, you ripped out her earring," the girl shrieked at me.

"Riki, I'm sorry," I choked out, trailing after her. I wasn't sure if she'd heard, so I said it again. No response. Her cousin wrapped her in a towel and they walked away, dripping and offended, and I didn't see her again until that evening, when our families gathered for supper. Riki was cool towards me but neither of us mentioned the incident again.

It's one of those memories that stays with you. But I still can't remember if Riki even knew how to swim.

My robot and I sat before the balcony doors and watched the night. Something like nostalgia stirred in me, and after a while my shoulders grew tense.

Our routine perpetuated itself. I plugged the robot in at night and grew distracted in my other tasks. The picture of Riki, which had been buried in a bottom drawer, took up new residence on my desk. Then I stopped going to work. My boss called me on the third day: "Hey Sparky, where the hell are you?" He sounded chipper as ever.

"I'm sick." I hung up.

There was an advertisement on the television set that I must have seen two dozen times a day. The newest gadget was coming soon and I'd better be the first in line to buy it. After all, we had to be able to stay connected. We *had to* be able to stay connected. "Soon," I said, looking

Robot Time Machines and the Fear of Being Alone

at my prophetic robot, "we'll all just live with computer chips in our brains and all we'll have to do to know a person is touch their bar code. Am I wrong?"

My robot beeped and blinked.

I used to live for the rare times Riki called me. I missed her when she wasn't around, and sometimes she wasn't around long enough that I would grow bitter and practice speeches about friendship and respect, promising myself I'd use them on her the next time we spoke. Of course, I never used them. So once upon a Friday night, long ago, the phone rang. I picked it up and heard only silence. I was about to hang up when I heard a shuffle, and then Riki's voice, passionless and sad. She asked if she could come over.

"I don't know," I said, glancing out the window. I was in a period of bitterness — I knew what it would be like if I said yes. She'd show up dripping rainwater, eyes swollen, holding a blue slush drink that contradicted the black mini dress and silver jewellery. She'd hug me for a stretch too long and walk all over my carpet in her wet high heels. I remembered when she kissed me that one night, deep and sloppy and tasting of synthesized raspberries. Or was it another night? Maybe she'd been wearing the yellow skirt with the slit up the side. Maybe she'd tasted of something a little harder than raspberries. When our bodies crushed together like that it was no different from the times she'd held me during thunderstorms and scary movies, the times I'd hugged her after a heartbreak, the times she'd hovered so close as I cooked her dinner and felt that she was more inside my space than anyone had ever been — I ached.

"Please?" Her voice cracked and crackled.

I shifted the phone against my ear and said, "Okay."

I stood by the balcony doors waiting. The sky moved fast and darkly, almost-invisible rain misting through streetlight beams. When I figured Riki would be getting close I went to the kitchenette to make a pot of coffee, even set out the milk and sugar for her. After thirty more minutes my fingers cramped up from being curled so tightly into fists. Of course she wouldn't show up. It was just like Riki to change her mind and forget to tell you.

An hour later I poured the coffee down the drain and went to bed. The city, with its lights and sirens, kept me awake, for a while.

That was months and months, transitioning into years, before I'd found my robot. Could I really have spent all that time alone? How did I manage to push it out of my mind for so long, to practically forget that conversation? Stretched out on my back on the living room floor with my robot companion pacing back and forth in front of the window I could think of nothing but my own damn throat squeezing out the word *Okay*. She'd been on her way to see me. She'd wound up on the six o'clock news instead. They showed a photograph of her smiling face next to footage of her car, ditched with its driver's-side door wide open and its nose in that Spring's flooded river. How alone she must have felt, how utterly and excruciatingly alone, as the water rushed in and pulled her away. *If* the water had rushed in and pulled her away.

She was listed as a missing person.

I was the only one who thought she was dead.

Afterwards I couldn't stop imagining her stretched out on a bed of water-logged weeds, petal dotted river water trickling around blue skin, blue nails, blue hair; I couldn't stop imagining her half hidden in writhing sea foam and miniature crab skeletons, wrapped in black kelp, buried beneath the snowy froth of gushing waterfalls, hair floating across her face in a bathtub filled to the rim, with bubbles clinging to the edges of her nostrils, with a glass of water perspiring on the floor.

I sat up and looked at the robot. "Why do you make me think of her so much?" I said. Its eyes glowed and its feet whirred, just the same as always. "Why do you remind me of her?" I hissed, and my fists came down with a muffled thud against the carpet. It wasn't enough. Anger rushed from my stomach up through my chest and out my arms. I grabbed the robot and hurled it against the wall. It clattered to the floor and rolled once, twice, awkward. It bleeped with alarm. I had almost forgotten her, I swear — she was almost nothing to me. And then I

Robot Time Machines and the Fear of Being Alone

found a robot half-buried at the edge of a creek near my apartment building and she came back to invade my skull the way she always did. I staggered to the robot and lifted it up again, staring into its lifeless face, professing all that lay before me, mocking me for what was gone. I smashed it once or twice against the wall and dropped its mangled body again. This time it lay motionless. The orange lights went out, and the whirring of its feet had died. I stood panting, staring.

It was noon on a Tuesday. I pressed my palms against my eyes. I choked, and my face burned. The apartment was too quiet, that's all — I was unnerved by the sudden and unfamiliar quiet.

. . .

I've gone back to work. Sometimes I wake with a jolt in the middle of the night and I'm in a ghost world, because I found a robot half buried at the edge of a creek near my apartment building and it showed me the death of something human. I peruse the abundance of inanimate objects and stare out across the city where no one touches, no one talks, no one's really there. This is prophecy: the moon hangs before me, just about to brush the side of the highrise across the street, never moving, never waxing, never waning.

FIMBULWINTER
J.J. Irwin

For his thirteenth birthday, Pyry's grandfather had promised to take him outside. They got as far as the airlock, audio from the external pick-ups filling the antechamber with the white-noise crackle and moan of the wind beyond the walls. They were just about to spin open the outer door when a voice joined the howling of the wind, then another voice, and another, a whole chorus of beautiful, terrible wailing. The boy hesitated, glanced up at his grandfather, but he knew there would be no adventuring now. The wolves were at the door, and that was that.

Still, he lingered in the airlock, unwilling to concede so quickly after months of anticipation.

"Pyry," his grandfather called, a few steps further down the corridor and already shucking his skinsuit and rebreather. "Pyry, come away from the door. There will be another day."

Fimbulwinter

The boy nodded reluctantly and braced to haul the door across. The wolves' voices chased along the corridor in staticky echo, "Pyry, Pyry."

He spun the airlock shut against the noise.

• • •

But the wolves didn't move on. Pyry roamed the corridors restlessly, listening to the audio at the airlocks for any sign of a change. He imagined sneaking out, evading the wolves somehow, seeing the world his parents used to talk so much about. He checked over the tables of seedlings in the hothouse for damage and signs of ill health, and pretended he had reached the nearby forest and found other people, hidden all this time. After he'd finished the last row he sat beneath the hydroponics tables and methodically tore a broken tomato leaf to pieces, and pretended he didn't hear Mr. Westola arguing with Ms. Laine.

"I tell you, Marco is ruining that boy with hope."

There was a hostile silence as Ms. Laine rummaged in a toolbox. She was mending the worn junction of one of the nutrient feeds, which had broken at last.

"Like you're doing any better with your moaning," she eventually growled. "At least one of us should have something to look forward to."

"What for? There's not a bit of difference we can make. Sometimes it feels like we're ants, and a mountain is sitting on us."

"A mountain *is* sitting on us, Westola. A hill, anyway."

They laughed, then fell silent again, but the timbre of the silence had changed to something more companionable. For several minutes the only sounds were the clunks and tapping of tools, and the occasional mutter or huffed breath as Ms. Laine wrestled with stiff connections.

"I want to see the sky again, Helka," said Mr. Westola, in a strange soft voice Pyry had never heard him use before.

LORE

Ms. Laine did not answer immediately. The metallic chirp of the ratchet echoed around the pipes near the ceiling.

"Bet it's bloody miserable out, Tuomo," she said at last, but it sounded too serious.

"Yeah," Mr. Westola sighed. "Miserable."

. . .

Pyry found his grandfather hunched broad-shouldered at the sampo in the kitchen, waiting for it to produce something for lunch. His dark eyes were fixed on the little door in the wall, chin jutted in concentration; whatever he was seeing, it clearly wasn't in the room.

"Vaari?"

His grandfather came back from whatever he was contemplating. "Hm? Eh, Pyry, you're like a ghost. Stop haunting the airlocks."

"There's nowhere else to be. You said we would go *outside*."

"Not with the wolves," his grandfather said, as implacable as the great steel door of an airlock.

"They aren't saying my name any more."

His grandfather's brow furrowed with affection. "Pyry, my boy. Not till they forget this place again. I will not risk losing you, too."

So it was his parents that put the weight in his grandfather's gaze today. More than three years since the wolves caught them outside, and every howl brought back memories of that day.

"I wish they'd go away," Pyry said. "I wish they'd just die." Instead of this endless reminder of what they'd lost.

"No. It's hard on us, but don't say that. One day things may be different."

Pyry sighed, and ducked his head as his grandfather ruffled his hair. The sampo pinged, and his grandfather opened the door on the wafting smell of pasties and pannu kakku. His grandfather must have programmed the sweet especially; the apology was a near-tangible thing in the air between them.

"Always one day, eh Marco?" said Mr. Westola lightly, coming in with a bowl of salad greens from the hothouses. He smiled, placed the bowl on the table. "Helka's just washing up."

"Just so," said his grandfather. The old man gave no indication of hearing Mr. Westola's tone, or indeed seeing his crooked smile, and Pyry wondered if it was just the return of the wolves which had sparked this new tension between them. But Ms. Laine came in, and they managed to get through lunch with no further barbs, so Pyry put it from his mind. Ms. Laine said she'd found the source of the fish tank leak on level three, and Mr. Westola talked about the new compounds he'd synthesised for the sampo, and Pyry's grandfather nodded and scowled at his plate in thought.

"Any news?" Ms. Laine asked carefully.

Pyry's grandfather glanced at him, then away. "Nothing. All frequencies. If I could just boost the signal —" He huffed out a breath. "Ah. It's not important. What do you say, Pyry, time for dessert?"

They finished lunch, and when Ms. Laine went to leave she asked Pyry to come feed the fish while she replaced the sump filters.

He swallowed a last bite of pannu kakku. "I'll be right with you."

The corridor was empty, as it always was now, but a low susurrus reached Pyry from the audio of the airlock at this end. He must have forgotten to switch it off the last time he checked. He hesitated with his fingers on the dial, listening to the crooning hiss, unable to tell at this volume if it was the wind or the wolves. At last he clicked it off and returned along the hallways.

As he passed the kitchen he heard his grandfather and Mr. Westola still talking —

"You shouldn't promise him those things, Marco. Even if we found a cure, we don't have the resources to distribute it. The world's too far gone."

LORE

"It doesn't have to cure the *world*, Westola."

— but he kept walking, fingers of one hand dragging a whisper with him along the walls.

• • •

When he dreamed, it was inverted — a half-heard whisper pulling him weightless through the corridors. Geometry twisted around him, so that the door to the hothouses led to the upper levels of the western arm of the complex. Even in his dream Pyry thought of it as the reclaimed end, though it had been many years since it was off-limits. The whisper became the buzz of a centrifuge, and Pyry rounded a corner into the labs, busy as they hadn't been since it was just Mr. Westola. Familiar figures worked at the benches, and the room was filled with half-remembered voices and the clean light of the generators at full power. He looked up at the people next to him, and his parents' faces smiled down upon him like a spotlight. They opened their smiling lips and said *we love you, Pyry*, but it sounded all wrong. Their mouths were gaping, and Pyry realised they were howling. Everyone was howling. The room was full of wolves.

• • •

He woke surrounded by a new sound, and it took several muzzy seconds before he could pinpoint what had tipped the world off-kilter. Ms. Laine's grim face at breakfast confirmed it.

"The air scrubber's going."

Pyry's grandfather scraped a hand over his rough cheeks, bleary-eyed. He would have been up all night in the comm room, sifting through the meaningless blatter and hiss of empty frequencies. "How long to fix it?"

"Can't."

In the stunned silence, the labouring gush of the usually-quiet air scrubber was like the wet catch of pneumonia in the lung.

"*Can't*, Laine, I've never heard you —"

"There must be some —"

"No!" Ms. Laine slapped her hand down on the table. Pyry couldn't remember the last time she'd yelled like that. She stared at each of them in turn, and her voice gentled. "There's no — This damned bunker. You can't run a facility this size with four people."

Pyry spoke into the lull. "How long?" Beside him, Mr. Westola half-turned in surprise. Too used to Pyry going silent during kitchen talks.

Ms. Laine dragged a hand through her hair. "I don't know. Not long. Maybe a few more months if we reduce the load on the system . . ."

"We could shut the peripherals down completely, route it all into, what? Hothouse, fish tanks, maybe two junctures either side of this pod?" Mr. Westola sketched quick shapes with the air as he spoke.

"Comm system. Your lab on three," said Pyry's grandfather. Mr. Westola shot him a look.

"I can keep the sampo ticking over with what can be made in the workroom near the tanks."

"But a cure —"

"Doesn't mean a thing if we're howling in here!"

"The point is," Ms. Laine broke over them, "this day was coming. The day when something important broke that we couldn't fix."

"So what do we do?" Pyry's grandfather, in a rare bout of consultation.

"Hell if I know. Start turning out the lights and putting up the chairs."

"Westola!"

"What? Do something, do nothing — it's only delaying the inevitable."

"Where was the last signal, Marco? What direction?"

"That was over six months ago, Laine. The chance of anyone —"

"It's a chance. One last roll of the dice. Once the air's gone, there's nothing for us here."

Pyry's grandfather subsided, conceding her point. "South, southwest. Oulu, maybe. I doubt there's anything for you at the other end, either."

Ms. Laine nodded, shrugged. "A risk."

"I never took you for a gambler before, Helka." Mr. Westola's smile took the bite out of the words. Ms. Laine smiled back.

・ ・ ・

They shut down the lower levels, the peripheral arms, retreating to the spine of the complex like some startled sea creature from Ms. Laine's vids. Pyry spent days helping to seal off the unused ducts, his small hands better able to reach into narrow vents. The ducts were smaller than he remembered, the angles sharper, like trying to squeeze into a shirt he'd outgrown. It felt like he'd outgrown the world, and when he banged his elbow and tore a long hole in his sleeve he didn't know whether to curse or cry.

He went to the laundry to get the sewing kit. Mr. Westola was sitting in the corridor outside next to a basket of clothes, sorting through which ones to take. Pyry picked over the scraps of thread in the kit, found a decent length and threaded up the needle. He took off his shirt and examined the hole. A straight rip, just the worn fabric giving up under pressure. Sew the edges back together and he'd have a bit more time before it needed to be patched.

Mr. Westola glanced up, and said, "If you need something to cannibalise, this pile's for salvage."

"I'm good. What did you mean, turning out lights and putting up chairs?" Pyry leaned against the door jamb while he worked.

Mr. Westola ran his thumb over the tattered collar of a woollen jumper, discarded it in favour of polarfleece. "It's what you do when you're the last person out. Tidy up. Leave it neat for the next day."

"The next day?"

"Or the next person. Whoever comes back."

Fimbulwinter

Pyry gave this some thought as he stitched his way along the hole, gently tugging it closed. "You think someone will come back here?"

For all his cynicism, Mr. Westola had always answered Pyry honestly. Now, for the first time, he saw a hesitation before the response. "Maybe, Pyry. It was a big world. You never know."

. . .

Through all the bustle of preparation his grandfather never mentioned leaving, didn't even pack anything from his quarters. Pyry was too busy to give it much thought, until something occurred to him late one night and he couldn't get back to sleep. He shuffled along the corridor, up a level to the comms room. The lights were off, and his grandfather sat illuminated by the dim blues and greens of the screens and control panels.

"Vaari, how will we all get past the wolves?" The problem he'd never figured out, for all his plans and dreaming.

His grandfather swivelled the chair around to look at him. His face was now backlit, almost invisible in the dark, but Pyry thought he seemed sad.

"I'm not going, Pyry. There needs to be someone to distract them."

There were unfamiliar emotions tangled in his grandfather's voice. Fear, resignation.

Longing — but not, Pyry thought, to leave. He crossed the few steps to stand next to the chair and pressed himself against his grandfather's side.

So this was the price of the gamble. To win against the wolves, somebody had to lose. Pyry stared at the screens that filled his grandfather's days and nights, that had promised a world beyond these walls but never delivered.

He'd imagined going outside, yes, but he'd always intended to return. Here was home. Family.

"I'll stay, too."

LORE

"Oh, Pyry." And when his grandfather ruffled his hair and left his hand resting on his head, Pyry didn't move away.

. . .

Ms. Laine and Mr. Westola headed out in the early hours one morning. Pyry's grandfather listened intently at the external audio feeds, tracking the ebb and flow of sound until he judged the wolves had circled past the southern exits. Then they donned skinsuits and rebreathers, and Mr. Westola fussed with his backpack while Ms. Laine gave Pyry and his grandfather a brisk hug.

"We'll send word — people — if we find anyone."

"Just wait, we'll mount a daring rescue," added Mr. Westola, and Pyry realised he was adjusting and readjusting his webbing because he was trying not to cry.

"Tuomo, Helka."

"Marco."

"Swift journey. Be safe."

"Goodbye, Pyry. Look after your vaari, yes?"

Pyry nodded. And now, absurdly, the tears came, blood-warm and damp beneath the weave of the skinsuit. Mr. Westola opened the outer door of the airlock. Sickly light seeped into the room and the wind shouldered through the gap, tugging and pushing at their bodies. Pyry's grandfather scanned the surroundings before gesturing the others through. Ms. Laine and Mr. Westola took off downslope towards the treeline, the twilit landscape swallowing their movements within a few hundred metres. Pyry and his grandfather struck out upslope, towards the entrance near the labs in the reclaimed end of the complex (now, technically, once again claimed by contamination from outside). Running towards the wolves. By his grandfather's reckoning, they should have just enough time to reach the airlock before the wolves could round the rubble of the building complex up here and see them, but the wind was even now delivering the sounds and scent of their uphill scramble.

Pyry had seen photos and vids of outside, but nothing had prepared him for the terrible void above him, the way the uneven floor seemed to stretch forever in every direction. He kept his eyes fixed on his shoes, trying to find safe footing, and concentrated on keeping pace with his grandfather's long strides. They were almost halfway to the door as the first wailing cries changed timbre and began to move closer. Pyry put on a burst of speed, his lungs straining against the measured delivery of the rebreather, concrete rubble shifting and slipping beneath his feet. In the brief-glimpsed distance he saw the wolves emerge around and over the shattered walls of the furthest building, but the unhemmed view made him feel nauseous; he focused on the bunker doorway of the airlock instead. But still his gaze slid to the familiar crowd, skittered back to the airlock. In the fragmented glances he saw the wolves pause in their stride, sensed the moment they chose to chase Pyry and his grandfather rather than that other, distant, trail. Ms. Laine and Mr. Westola were free. Relief surged through him, damping his adrenaline, and Pyry couldn't keep from grinning.

Beside him his grandfather faltered, the rubble skidding out from under his feet; he scraped down the edge of a jutting slab of concrete before he could catch himself. He was up and running again in moments, but the damage was already done. He fell again, and as Pyry bent to drag him up he saw the laddered rip in his grandfather's skinsuit, gaping like an airlock thrown open. Outside was already flooding in.

His grandfather spasmed and curled in on himself like a withered leaf. Then he was clawing madly at the skinsuit, and he tore the rebreather from his face, mouth gasping like the fish did as he sucked more air inside. A high-pitched noise keened from his throat, a weak echo of the cries descending upon them, and Pyry realised the danger. He staggered out of range of his not-grandfather's flailing hand, broke into a stumbling sprint for the last few meters to the airlock. The wind was full of the wolves' chorus, joyful cries of "Marco! Pyry!" He slammed the door shut as another familiar voice began calling his name.

• • •

Pyry had never been afraid of the dark, but now he found himself turning on every light as he walked from room to room. The corridors seemed strange, their geometry subtly changed from what he knew so that everywhere was new and unsettling. The hydroponics and the fish tanks hummed through their automatic cycles, but without the casual bickering of Mr. Westola and Ms. Laine the rooms seemed louder somehow. Harsher. The gurgling breath of the air scrubber reminded him too clearly of his grandfather writhing on the broken floor of outside. He ate whatever it was the sampo produced, but the only thing he remembered about the meal was that it took more effort to chew.

Almost without thinking, Pyry wandered to the comms room. The conversation with his grandfather seemed so long ago. He settled into the chair his grandfather would sit in, and stared for a long, unblinking moment at the array of blank-eyed screens. His grandfather had powered most of it down while he was gone, and though Pyry knew he could bring it all to wakefulness again, the dark and silence made his chest feel hollowed out.

A small-screened pad lay tucked in the far corner of the desk. Pyry pulled it towards him, turned it on, and found himself meeting the smiling eyes of his parents. The lighting was strange, the walls a crisp blue he couldn't place; it took a few slippery seconds before he realised this was a photo from before. The funny lighting was the sun; the walls were not walls at all, but the sky (he swallowed the taste of bile, remembering the great emptiness above him as he ran). His father's hair was streaked paler, his skin darker; his mother wore a colourful, lumpy beanie he'd never seen, dark eyes the same as her father's crinkling up at the corners. Pyry thought of the half-glimpsed figures leaping closer as he ran for the airlock, the way his eye had been drawn despite his fear. Had he seen them, or was it wishful thinking?

He scrolled through his grandfather's photo album, ignoring the tags and annotations in favour of the faces, the moments captured. There were a lot of photos from before, above ground, and Pyry tried to imagine what his grandfather was thinking as he sat in this chair and pored over the album and waited for a message from the outside world.

At last he fell into a fitful sleep propped up in the chair. When he woke with a sore neck and the uneasy conviction there was a whisper sliding in somewhere on the edge of his hearing, Pyry stalked through all the corridors and rooms and made sure every single audio feed of outside was turned off.

· · ·

Ms. Laine had been right, of course: the complex was too large for four people to keep running. It was far too large for Pyry. When a pump switch in the hothouses stopped working, he had no idea what to do. His grandfather had always fixed the electricals. As that block of greens began to look more and more yellow, the lack of human voices pressed like a rough lump of concrete rubble on his heart. He turned the external audio back on. It was better than the emptiness, the bronchial cough of the air scrubber and the muted hum of electrical systems on the brink of collapse. Better than the sense that the complex — the world — was hovering on the edge of a sleep that could only be measured in the slow cycle of mortar and metal, and only Pyry had been left shut out and awake.

He began to understand why Mr. Westola wanted to see the sky, to escape the dying body of the complex one more time before the end. He wondered if Ms. Laine and Mr. Westola had reached safety somewhere, or if it was just another slow fall in a different place. Or perhaps they were howling outside now, too.

Not here, though. He recognised every voice keeping him companion.

• • •

It took a while for him to decide, even so. On the final day he programmed pasties and pannu kakku from the sampo, ate the meal with deliberation at the empty kitchen table. Powered down what systems he could. Last person out.

"Turning out the lights and putting up the chairs," he murmured, but there was no one to respond.

He debated leaving a message in case someone came back one day. Eventually he placed his grandfather's photo album in the centre of the kitchen table, on top of a carefully-penned note: *Going out to see the sky*. He didn't sign it. The two people left to care would recognise his writing.

The airlock door didn't want to open, and Pyry had to throw his whole weight to shove it along its tracks and repeat the struggle to close it when he was on the other side. The effort disrupted his plans for a smooth, confident exit. He reached the outer door breathing heavily, adrenaline curdling his stomach and sending a wash of tingles through his veins with every thudding heartbeat. He took a few calming breaths and reached for the handle.

They were waiting for him on the other side. Pyry picked out his grandfather in the pressing, carolling throng that pulled him over the threshold into its embrace, saw the half-remembered faces of those who had gone or been taken by the outside over the years, some he hadn't seen since childhood. His parents, strong and strange as all the wolves were, impervious to the wind as it whipped the tattered remnants of their clothes. He breathed deeply, feeling the taint of outside burning over his skin, buzzing in his lungs and through his blood. He

Fimbulwinter

raised his gaze to the vast expanse of the sky, the land rolled out around them, and lifted his voice to join the wolves, wordless, joyful.
    To howl.
    To sing the beauty of the broken world.

ON THE MAKING OF A DEAD MAN'S HAND
George R. Galuschak

When the Shoggoth ate the last goldfish I didn't have anything else to feed it, so I bundled up and went out into the streets of Arkham. Cold April night, one of those nights that feel like winter's here to stay, winter will never end. A butter-yellow moon waxed, gibbous, casting pale light on the empty sidewalks.

I went to the grocery store on Innsmouth Street. The place stank of stale vegetables and spoiled cat food, but it stayed open past midnight. I passed the racks of comic books and lurid detective magazines and picked out three cans of chicken soup. The Shoggoth loved chicken soup and would slurp it down, noodles and all.

I was walking to the register when I saw her, shivering in the aisle, looking lost. She was crying, the tears dripping down her cheeks. Her name was Katie. I knew her from school. She was in Unspeakable Horrors, an undergrad class I was auditing. She sat next to the door and never spoke.

On the Making of a Dead Man's Hand

I could have just passed her. I didn't need the hassle: late Tuesday night, three cans of chicken soup in hand, the store about to close. A bunch of ungraded exams and an unfinished dissertation awaited me at home.

Instead I stopped. I cleared my throat. I said, "Are you okay?"

"I'm fine." And then her eyes rolled back in her head and she collapsed into the canned marshmallows and corn syrup. I made a grab for her and got her under the arms and the cans of chicken soup clattered to the floor and the Pakistani who owned the grocery store glared at me and it looked like a scene out of some cheap black-and-white melodrama, me catching the swooning damsel. I felt like a fool.

She pushed herself away from me. "Sorry."

"That's okay," I said. "Are you all right?"

She shook her head. "I don't want to be alone."

"Oh. Well." I cleared my throat. "Maybe a cup of tea would make you feel better? I don't live very far from here."

"I'd like that, Henry," she said, smiling. So she knew my name. I wasn't sure.

We went back to my apartment. I live in a loft on the third floor of a bakery. It's a small, cramped space, a niche within a niche, an example of Lovecraftian geometry if I ever saw one: it exists, but makes no sense.

I put the soup away. When I turned back, Katie was sitting on the bed, taking in my loft. A girl on my bed; there's a first time for everything. I filled the hot pot with water for tea: chamomile. My hands were shaking when I handed her the cup. If she noticed she didn't comment.

"Thank you." She brushed straw-colored hair from her face. Her ears were still red from the cold. "I'm having a really bad day, Henry."

"I'm sorry." I looked round my loft. Where should I sit?

"I need a Dead Man's Hand. You don't happen to have one, do you?"

LORE

"I'm afraid not." I sat next to her on the bed. She didn't shriek or throw the contents of her teacup into my face. Instead she put her head on my shoulder.

I hesitated, for just a moment, and then I put my arm around her waist. My heart was pounding so loud I could hardly hear her talking, that is, I knew she was speaking, muttering under her breath, her lips forming words, but I had no idea what she was saying, and then it was too late.

I froze. Literally.

Katie scrambled off the bed. When she reached for her purse she knocked over her cup and hot tea spilled all over the hardwood floor.

"Oh shit," she muttered, pulling out a pair of scissors. And then she turned back to me.

"Go to sleep," she said, and I fell back onto the bed.

• • •

At two a.m. the Shoggoth started to moan, the thin, soft wail of a human infant. When I turned on the night lamp I saw hair clippings on my pillow.

"Henry, what is it?" Katie sat bolt upright. She grabbed my arm. "It sounds like a baby."

"It's okay." I stumbled out of bed, poured a can of soup into a pot and brought it to the hot plate. Waited for it to heat.

"It's a Shoggoth, isn't it?" Katie shivered. "There are rumors all over the department."

"Yes, it's a Shoggoth." I dumped the soup into the fish tank. Little mouths opened and closed, making cooing noises. Eyes — cat, goat, lizard — blinked, looked at me. Tendrils reached up, brushed my fingers. "And it's a pain in the ass."

On the way back to bed I stepped in a puddle. I reached down, touched the wet floor, brought my fingers to my nose: chamomile.

On the Making of a Dead Man's Hand

Something niggled at the back of my head, something I couldn't quite recall.

"Come back to bed, Henry." Katie said. "I'm cold."

When I climbed into bed, the hairs were gone from my pillow. I put my arm around Katie. We lay next to each other. I could tell by her breathing that she wasn't sleeping.

. . .

The next day: after my Cthulhoid Logic seminar I didn't go to the library to prepare for my lectures. The exams went unmarked. I went to the five-and-dime for a goldfish run and when I opened my apartment door there was Katie, putting away groceries, like she belonged.

"Hi there." We kissed on the lips.

I fed the Shoggoth a goldfish. Katie cooked. We ate dinner — pork chops with mashed potatoes and green beans. After we washed the dishes I put my arm around her waist.

"Let's go to bed," I said.

Katie gave me a strained smile. Nodded. It didn't go well. During lovemaking she pushed me away and ran to the bathroom. She stayed there for a long time. When she came out her eyes were raw and puffy.

"What's wrong?" I reached out for her. "Are you okay?"

"I'm fine." She brushed my hands away. "No big deal."

"Was it me? Did I hurt you?"

"Drop it. Please." Katie slipped into bed. When I touched her shoulder she rolled away. I lay next to her, trying to figure out what I'd done. Finally she said, "I'm not a good person, Henry."

"Who is?" I put my arm around her, and she let me. "What does being a good person mean, anyway? I've never been able to figure that one out."

"I'm a witch."

"That's what I thought. Are you doing the Generalist track, or did you specialize?"

LORE

Katie laughed. "You've got a funny way of looking at things."

"I know I'm not good at this," I told her. "I haven't had much — uh, practice. But I'll get better and — "

"Be quiet, Henry." She rolled into me and it was all right, just like that. We made love and this time it was good.

Afterwards she said, "I need a Dead Man's Hand. And I'm just an undergrad, it's way beyond my skills. Will you help me?"

"Of course. I'll do whatever you want. You know that."

Katie flushed. She looked away, towards the fish bowl. The Shoggoth was putting on a show, writhing and twisting, glowing green and red and orange like a lava lamp. It did that after it ate, sometimes.

"What's the story with the Shoggoth?" she asked.

"There's a little museum in Arkham. The remains of the Dyer expedition are stored there." When she looked blank I said, "They discovered a Shoggoth colony in Antarctica. The museum's full of dogsleds, old parkas, mummified giant penguins. A bunch of useless old junk, except it's all brimming with Shoggoth particulates. Inert, of course. I scraped off a sample and dumped it into a bowl of hot chicken soup and bone marrow. It grew."

Katie shivered. "Why would you do that?"

"It was going to be my final project, back when I was an undergrad. And then I realized I couldn't use it. I'd get expelled. The faculty members here are very conservative, you know. So now it just keeps me company."

"Should you let it run around free like that?"

"I don't like imprisoning anything." She looked stricken, like I'd hurt her somehow, so I changed the subject. "I'll start on your Dead Man's Hand tomorrow."

"Maybe it's not a good idea." Katie spoke the words slowly. "It's not fair of me, to take up your time this way. I know you're awful busy."

I looked at my empty apartment, at the blank walls, at the chipped and peeling paint. Water stains on the ceiling from a busted pipe.

On the Making of a Dead Man's Hand

Flecks of plaster littered the floor. Nietzsche said: *When you look into the void it looks back at you.* Maybe he'd been to my apartment.

I said, "For you, I'll make the time."

.   .   .

There are a lot of misconceptions about a Dead Man's Hand. Some people still call it a Hand of Glory. Dead Man's Hand is a better term. You dig up the body of a murderer and chop off his hand — nothing glorious about it. The nails must be long. A number of chants and invocations need to be said over the severed hand: Latin, Greek, Arabic, corrupt Coptic. Proper enunciation of the syllables is essential.

The murderer doesn't need to be hanged: any old killer will do. The part about making a candle from the body fat is bunk. No candle is needed. If manufactured properly, blue flames will spout from the hand's fingernails. It's quite a sight.

A Dead Man's Hand will render the bearer invisible. It cannot open locked doors or induce paralysis. A Dead Man's Hand is a necessity for major summonings because it acts as a beacon to the summoned being; one must take precautions to ensure that the entity does not eat the hand, and then the summoner.

The problem, of course, is finding a murderer. The ingredients are hard to come by since Massachusetts discontinued the death penalty. There are ways, though; there are always ways.

.   .   .

A week passed. I gathered the ingredients. It wasn't hard. I bought the goggles at a hardware store, made a few trips to the local slaughterhouse and I was done.

The hardest part was finding a blender, because I don't own one. Finally I snuck into the Faculty Break Room and used the blender there. It pulverized the concoction of hair and bone and other things into a

LORE

foul-smelling paste, which I smeared all over the lenses. I buried the goggles in the park at midnight and said the incantations over them. I used the word *morthor*, Middle English for murder. It seemed right.

I'd found the spell in my undergrad years, when I'd worked at the Arkham Library. It was in a very old book, spine cracked, ink faded, pages like dried leaves. *A spell for seeing things best not seen*, the text read. Just what I wanted.

When I dug up the goggles three nights later, the lenses had a greenish tinge. I wrapped them in a towel and kept them in the dark.

We were ready for the graveyard.

. . .

"Here you go, Joe." I set down the cardboard carrier. "You like your coffee light and sweet, right?"

"Thanks a lot, Henry." We stood in Joe's security hut, stationed next to the gates of Arkham Cemetery. Joe's eyes were fixed on a 12-inch TV, where an episode of *Cheers* was playing. "Did they have any cream donuts?"

"Yeah. I got you a few. So what's it like out there?"

"Pretty quiet," Joe said. He reached into the bag and pulled out a donut. "Clean up after yourself, and watch out for the ghouls." He laughed.

"Okay, thanks a lot." I turned to go.

"That's Katie Mews out there, right? Why didn't she come in with you?"

"She's a bit shy."

"What are you guys doing, anyway?"

"Gathering materials," I told him. "She needs a Dead Man's Hand."

"What for?"

"I have no idea. She didn't tell me."

"Huh." Joe suddenly seemed a lot more interested. "Is she your girlfriend?"

On the Making of a Dead Man's Hand

I shrugged.

"It's complicated, right?" He laughed. "I know the feeling. So why don't you just ask her? About the hand, I mean."

I didn't say anything.

"Are you okay, man?" Joe was a grad student, also. I'd read some of his thesis: quantum physics and time travel.

"Fine. Why do you ask?"

"Watch yourself, that's all. You meet her brother yet?"

"No."

"He's a nut. We were in a few classes together, before he got expelled. He founded that fertility cult, the one that — "

I made a show of looking at my watch. "I've got to go, Joe."

He nodded. I went outside.

Arkham graveyard: midnight. It was raining, drizzle morphing to wet snow. Katie stood under a tree. With the hood of her parka up she looked like an Eskimo. She was shivering, her face white as a snowflake.

"What's wrong?" I asked her. "Are you cold?"

"Are you kidding?" She looked at me like I was out of my mind. "We're in a graveyard, Henry. In the middle of the night."

"Let's get moving." When you've been in as many cemeteries as me they all look alike.

Graveyards are like towns. They have good sections and bad sections. We headed straight for the bad section, the unhallowed ground, the place where they buried the wicked. The grave markings got cheaper and cheaper, marble headstones and crosses to wooden stakes jammed into the earth like fence spokes to black stones covered with moss.

"Good enough," I said. We stopped in front of a skeletal willow tree.

"What now?" Katie dropped her shovel to the earth and flinched at the clunking sound it made.

"Put these on." I turned off the flashlight and rummaged for the goggles. They sat in my backpack, heavier since we'd entered the graveyard.

"What do they do?"

"Trust me." I'd tested the goggles the night before, in front of a mirror. They'd worked. "Just put them on."

LORE

"Okay." She looked at me for a long moment before putting them over her eyes. "Now what?"

"We wait." I sat under the tree. Katie hunkered next to me and put her head on my shoulder. It felt good. I closed my eyes, just for a moment, and thought of the two of us in my creaky bed.

Katie's cry woke me. It wasn't loud, but it was enough. My eyes opened. She stood rigid against the willow tree, hands over her cheeks, staring at something I couldn't see.

"Take off the goggles," I said. The ground was wet and cold and slick; when I got up I almost fell on my ass.

"Do you see him?" Her voice rose. "Do you?"

"It's okay." I pulled the goggles off Katie's head and threw them onto the grass.

"I fell asleep," she said. "When I woke I felt stiff so I got up, to walk it off. That's when I saw him. He was looking at me — no, he was leering at me. It was dark, but I could see him. It's like he was lit up from behind. He was dressed like a homeless person. He had a big bald white head. He spread his hands and they were huge – his fingernails were black. And then he spoke."

"What did he say?"

"Don't know." She shook her head. "I didn't hear. Or maybe I did hear and I blocked it out."

"Forget about it." I hefted the shovels. "Show me where he appeared."

The grave: a grassless mound, ground covered with lichen. I scraped at it with the edge of the shovel, peered at the black stone underneath. Touched it with my bare fingers: cold, so cold. No markings.

"Dig." I handed her a shovel. "I'll help, but it needs to start with you."

"Who was he?" Katie drove the shovel into the earth. Her shoulders made a little shuddery movement, and a chunk of dirt flew through the air.

"I'll tell you later." I picked up a shovel. "No more talking. Let's finish this."

On the Making of a Dead Man's Hand

We dug. Two hours later Katie's shovel hit rotten wood. Widening the hole took another hour. When we pried off the lid, the smell hit. Katie cried out, pulled herself from the hole and rushed off.

The body lay in its cheap pine coffin, arms crossed over its chest. Moss grew on the pauper's suit. I pinched the hand. It was in perfect condition, the skin rough and leathery, with a great set of Fu Manchu nails.

I heard Katie, creeping back.

"I've got a hacksaw in the bag," I told her. "Go get it."

A wet, snuffling grunt; something cold and gritty touched the back of my neck. I turned and swung the shovel. It connected. I caught a glimpse of eyes, a pair of yellowing tusks, and then the thing leaning over the grave squealed and galloped off.

I hefted myself out of the hole. Katie was nowhere in sight. I called her name once, twice, three times, and then I saw her, walking towards me, wiping her mouth with her hands.

"Where the hell were you?"

"Sorry. I didn't want you to see me getting sick. I got lost, coming back." Her voice trembled. "God, I'm such a wimp."

"No you aren't." I didn't mention the ghoul. They're harmless enough — tap them on the nose with a shovel and they run off — but why freak her out even more? "Bring my bag."

We didn't have any problems after that.

•   •   •

Three days later I sat in my apartment, waiting for Katie. With my guidance she'd cast the final invocation the night before. I glanced at my watch: ten minutes since the last time I'd looked.

The Shoggoth reared halfway out of the fish tank. Golden wings formed, molted, melted. Mouths opened; the song of a thousand cicadas filled the air. When I brought over a goldfish it brushed itself against my hand, its pseudopods tickling my fingers like nibbling fish mouths.

LORE

The Shoggoth swallowed the goldfish whole.

It said, "Henry."

Its voice was flat, atonal.

I jumped away from the fish tank like it was on fire. Backpedaled until the backs of my knees hit the bed. Sat. The Shoggoth watched me. A pair of giant lips formed, parted. I heard Katie's voice, in the throes of orgasm. "Henry. Oh Henry."

The front door opened and closed. Katie walked in.

"Hi there." She looked at my flushed face. "What's up? Are you okay?"

"I'm fine." I glanced at the fish tank, but all was silent. Shoggoths are great mimics. That's all it was doing, mimicking her voice. I went to Katie. We kissed.

"Where have you been?" I asked her.

"Doing this and that. Is the hand ready?"

"Let's see." I opened the fridge and pulled out the Dead Man's Hand, wrapped in butcher's paper. Spoke the invocation. Held it up. "Can you see me?"

"You look like a smudged blur. I can tell something's there, but I can't make out what."

"Needs a few more hours." I put the hand back into the fridge and rubbed my own hands together. "Why don't we celebrate?"

We went to Donnie's, a student joint. It was small, a bar with a pool table and dartboard in one room, a dining area with a bunch of booths in the other. We ordered a pizza and a pitcher of beer, sat at a booth and talked; or rather, I talked. Katie didn't feel like talking.

Finally she said, "Don't you want to know why I need a Dead Man's Hand, Henry?"

"I assume you want to vanish." I refilled my mug. "That's all a Dead Man's Hand is good for. Unless you want to summon an Elder God."

"I'd like that." She smirked when I paused in mid-sip. "Vanishing, I mean."

"You'd be all alone, then."

"There are worse things than being alone."

On the Making of a Dead Man's Hand

"Maybe, but I'll take my chances." I exhaled, not quite drunk enough yet. "When am I going to meet your brother?"

Katie's eyes widened, and then narrowed. "When did I mention my brother?"

"You've talked about him before. Don't you remember?"

"No." She shook her head. "My brother is a troubled man, Henry. But he's all the family I've got."

Our waitress came, bearing pizza. We stopped talking for a while. I polished off the pitcher, ordered another.

"My goodness," Katie watched me drain yet another beer. "I didn't know you drank like this."

"Alcohol is a social lubricant." I put down my mug. "It's also an effective way of countering control spells."

"Oh." Her face turned white. Her mouth opened and nothing came out.

I reached over, plucked Katie's purse from her lap and opened it. I found the lock of hair, tied in a ring and tucked inside an envelope, and held it over the candle. Greasy flames shot up, and then the knot was gone. I brushed ash from my fingers.

"You enchanted me," I said. "Took a lock of my hair our first night together and made a Lover's Knot."

"When did you know?" Her voice was a husky whisper.

"For sure? When I tested the goggles in the mirror. It was quite a sight, let me tell you."

Katie stood up. Her chair clattered to the floor.

I took her hand. "Sit down."

"Let go of me, Henry." Her face looked frozen.

"Sit down. Please. Why don't you tell me about it? Maybe I can help."

"Nobody can help me."

"Maybe, maybe not. We won't know until you tell me."

Katie's face worked. She sat back down. "I'm surprised you'll even talk to me, after what I did."

LORE

"You didn't hurt anybody." I spoke slowly because I was drunk and I didn't want to say anything stupid. "I don't have a girlfriend or a wife. I fell in love with a beautiful woman, that's all."

She flushed. "I used you."

"You needed help. You felt like you didn't have any other choice." I put my hand over hers. "I know you felt bad about it."

"I did it for my brother." Katie was crying, big fat blobs running down her cheeks. "He needs a Dead Man's Hand for his fertility cult, the Coven of the Dark Wood." She put her head in her hands. "I'm so sorry, Henry."

"Sorry for what?" The words slipped out before I could stop them. "I'm not that awful in bed, am I?"

"Of course not."

"Good. You've got a Dead Man's Hand now. Give it to him. He'll go away and then we can be together."

"It's not that easy."

"Why not?" I raised my voice. "Why can't it be that easy? I'm sick of hanging out in graveyards. Why can't we do things like drink coffee in bed and then get under the sheets?"

"I killed my parents, Henry."

I shut up.

Katie opened her mouth and the words came tumbling out.

"I was just a girl, five or six years old. We lived in a farm way out in the boondocks. My parents had this little white goat they kept penned up. I was in charge of taking care of him. He was such a sweet little thing. I spent a lot of time playing with that goat, because I didn't have any friends.

"My parents had a party one Halloween. At least I thought it was a party. People came from the surrounding farms. They took off their clothes and went out into the cow field and started chanting and singing. A hot wind blew across the plains. It stank. Clouds formed on the horizon. Thunder rumbled.

On the Making of a Dead Man's Hand

"My father told me to get the goat. He stood before an altar, and he had a big terrible black knife in his hand. My mother was next to him. Everyone else stood back. When I got to the pen, the goat was terrified. I opened the gate and he came running out. He butted against me, bleating and trembling. He was my friend, Henry. So I undid his harness and let him go. He galloped off into the woods. I hid in the barn, because I was so scared."

"And then the thing — it took my parents. Instead of the goat."

"I see." I swallowed. My throat was dry. I felt stone cold sober, as if all the alcohol had been squeezed out of me. "The Coven of the Dark Wood. Your brother posted their creed and summoning chant on the school wiki last year. Did you know that?"

She shook her head. Tears ran down her cheeks.

"It's still there. I read it last night. Their summoning chant is a variant of an older chant, passed down by oral tradition by the hill folk of Tennessee and Virginia. It's obviously what your parents used. And it's rubbish. Hogwash. Their math is abominable."

"Is math important when you're doing a summoning?" She had trouble getting the words out. "I thought all you needed was a Dead Man's Hand and a — a sacrifice."

"Yes, math is important. The Great Old Ones don't care about creed. It's all about math. What do you think music is, Katie? It's audible math. Why do you think I spent hours coaching you on the right way to chant the invocation? Certain syllables have to be stressed, certain notes must be hit. The Great Old Ones always follow the rules. They are sticklers for the rules."

She wiped her eyes. "Do they have to?"

"Who knows? But they do. Even Cthulhu did." I shrugged. "Their summoning chant is so riddled with errors that the only time it would have a hope in hell of succeeding would be on Halloween or Walpurgis Night. They might summon something, then, and it would gobble up its summoners and go back to whence it came."

"Really?"

"Really. Their summoning chant has no safeguards or protections. Your parents were so focused on opening the gate they didn't give any thought to controlling what came through. It's a common mistake amateurs make." I grabbed Katie's hand and squeezed it. "What happened to your parents was not your fault."

"It's not my fault." Katie repeated the words. She wasn't crying anymore. Her eyes narrowed. She squeezed my hand so hard it hurt.

"Let's go home," I said.

Katie nodded. She shifted and blurred before my eyes. We paid the bill and went out, into the cold night air. I threw up in the first handy alley and passed out at the next.

• • •

Blurry voices, head spinning. My eyelids fluttered. I cracked open my eyes, looked around. I lay in bed, in my apartment, fully clothed. The ceiling whirled.

I raised my head. Saw a man standing next to Katie in the kitchen. A young Charlie Manson, dirty sweatshirt and jeans, long black hair, eyebrows like unshaved armpits.

"Can't you shut that thing up?" Charlie snarled. The Shoggoth was croaking like a bullfrog.

Katie muttered something I didn't hear. Her face looked like a storm cloud about to break.

"Don't talk to your brother like that," he barked. "Now get your things. We're going. We'll take this fool with us. He may have his uses."

"Too late." Katie crossed her arms. "He burned the Lover's Knot."

"Make another, then." He laughed. "You'll be doing him a favor."

"Hold on." Katie opened the fridge and pulled out the Dead Man's Hand. She held it up. "It's finally done. Do you like it?"

"Of course." Charlie nodded. "We need a beacon to complete the Summoning."

"Take it then." Katie's lip curled back. She swung the Dead Man's Hand like a baseball bat. It hit Charlie square in the face. He backpedaled, fell on his ass.

On the Making of a Dead Man's Hand

"Here you go." Katie threw the hand at him. He ducked, and it hit the cabinet. "Get out of here and don't come back. Tell Cthulhu I said hi."

"What's wrong with you?"

"What's wrong with me?" Katie's voice rose. "You're what's wrong with me. You lied to me. You've been lying to me my whole life."

"About what?" Charlie tried to look bewildered, did a bad job of it.

"It's not my fault their shitty spell didn't work," she shrieked. "It's not my fault they didn't know what they were doing."

"Did he tell you that?" Charlie glared at me. "That's a lie. It — "

"Why did you need him to make a Dead Man's Hand?" Katie spat the words out. "Why didn't you make one yourself, if you're such hot shit?"

Charlie's mouth opened. "I didn't — "

"You didn't know how to make one, that's why." She laughed. "You don't even know how to activate the thing." She picked up the Dead Man's Hand and waved it in his face. "Go on. Say the invocation. Vanish."

"Stop it." He snatched the hand from her. "I'm warning you."

"You lied to me. You told me I killed my parents and I believed you. You made me whore myself off. Because you don't know shit."

There was a moment of silence, broken by the sound of the Shoggoth rearing halfway out of the fish tank. And then Charlie sprang to his feet. I heard his fist smack against her face, and then I was up on my feet. I staggered into the kitchen. Katie lay on the floor, face in her hands. Charlie reached out to her, his face white.

He said: "Katie, I'm sorry. I didn't mean to — "

"Get away from her." That's what I meant to say, but what came out was gibberish.

"You." Charlie turned to me, his bug eyes ablaze. "This is your fault."

Suddenly there was a knife in his hand: hocus-pocus. I stared at it, shocked. He swung it. I staggered back, watched a black button fall to the floor. Put a hand to my belly. My best flannel shirt was split to the skin. I held the ends in my hands, tried to repair the tear.

Charlie reared back, snarling, the knife in his hand.

"No don't," Katie shrieked. "Please don't — "

The Shoggoth launched itself from the fish tank and landed at Charlie's feet. Thud. A mouth formed. Lips parted. I saw a set of white, even, perfect teeth.

"Hi there," it said.

The Shoggoth's lips puckered. It puffed up, like an angry cat, and engulfed him. The knife fell from Charlie's fingers. He was dead before it hit to the ground.

Katie looked at me, her mouth forming a perfect O. She got to her feet and threw her arms around my waist. I touched her hot face, felt the bruise on her cheek. We staggered away from the kitchen and tumbled onto the bed. The Shoggoth slithered back to the fish tank. Its movements were slow, sluggish. It looked very full.

"It killed him. The bastard. Good." Katie's face was exultant, and then it crumpled. "Oh my God."

She put her head in her hands. Her shoulders heaved. The storm broke.

I put my arms around her.

Held on.

• • •

"Henry." A hand, shaking my shoulder. "Wake up, Henry."

"What's the matter?" I cracked open my eyes. Morning: light trickled in through the windows. My head thumped like a leaky tuba and there was an awful taste in my mouth.

"We've got a visitor," Katie said.

I sat up. The Shoggoth towered over the bed, a cone-shaped mass of lips and mouths and eyes shifting in and out of existence. My gorge rose.

On the Making of a Dead Man's Hand

"Could you not do that, please?" I asked, and the waterfall of facial features stopped.

"What are we going to do, Henry?" Katie hugged the sheets to her chest.

"Make coffee." I got to my feet, tottered towards the hot plate. "Coffee will make everything better."

The Shoggoth followed me into the kitchen. It was quite a bit bigger than it had been the night before. When I opened the cupboard, the coffee can fell out of my hands and clattered to the floor. The Shoggoth reached out with a pseudopod and picked it up. Three more pseudopods formed. It poured water, scooped coffee grinds and opened the fridge, all at the same time.

"Be careful with the mix," I said. "I like my coffee good and strong. One spoonful per cup."

The Shoggoth ignored me. Watching it made me dizzy so I lurched back to bed and collapsed. I closed my eyes and listened to the sound of the surf pounding through my skull. And then someone pinched my nose. Hard.

"Get up." Katie said. She pinched harder.

"Ow." I opened my eyes. "What's wrong?"

"That thing is eight feet tall, Henry." Katie spoke in the smooth, even tones of a person about to lose their shit.

"Yeah, it's big." I put a hand over my eyes and looked at the Shoggoth. "You know, it's not black. It's constantly shifting colors. I never noticed that before."

"Maybe you can ask why it does that," Katie suggested. "Before it eats us."

"Don't be silly." I watched the Shoggoth come out of the kitchen, holding a pair of steaming mugs in its pseudopods. I took a mug. "Thank you."

The Shoggoth patted my foot.

Katie took a cautious sip of her own mug. "Hey, good coffee."

"Can you talk?" I asked the Shoggoth.

A mouth formed. "Talk," it piped in that same atonal voice.

"Yes, that's right." I sipped my coffee. It was good and strong, just the way I liked it.

"I talk," the Shoggoth said. "Just like Henry."

"Very good."

A series of mouths formed. "Talk talk talk talk talk talk talk talk talk talk talk talk talk," it babbled.

I raised my voice. "My head hurts." The Shoggoth shut up and watched us drink our coffee.

"What do you want?" I asked when it didn't go away.

"Hungry," it said.

"Don't look at us," Katie said.

"All right, then." I went to the feeder bowl and gave the Shoggoth a goldfish and that seemed to make it happy. It couldn't squeeze itself back into the fish tank so I led it to the bathtub. It fit, barely. When I came out Katie was leaning against her pillow. She handed me my coffee mug.

"Is it going to be okay?"

"I think so." From the bathroom came the sound of sparrows chirping. "Yes. It's doing bird calls, which means it's in a good mood."

"Don't you ever get scared, Henry?"

"Of course. That night you came to my apartment I was terrified. Had no idea where to sit."

"That was so cute." And then her face fell. She shook her head.

"I'm sorry about your brother," I told her.

"So am I." Katie hesitated, and then spoke. "Henry…"

I took a sip of coffee. "Yes?"

She patted the sheets. "Get under here."

GHOST
Bear Weiter

She saw the eyes first — pale, ringed in red, and wide with fear. He was an albino boy, a couple of years younger than herself, huddled within the low foliage between twin tree trunks. Mud coated his luminous skin and his chest surged in search of breath.

From all around thrashing could be heard and closing in fast. It was a violent sound reserved for clearing — or searching.

Makia was bright. She was the granddaughter of Shasheeni, the only witch within a few days walk, and Makia did the bulk of the herb gathering for her. She was young, but as Grandmother lived outside of any tribes, Makia had learned how to survive in the forest surrounded by assorted peoples.

She knew immediately — hunters were searching for the albino boy.

"Stay quiet," she said in the dominant tongue. The northern tribe was from across the river but also the most populous, treating all lands as their own. Seeing no reaction she placed her finger across her lips. He nodded to that.

A man crashed into her small clearing. He was tall, lean, and carried a short spear in one hand. Across his bronzed brow were three horizontal stripes of white — a mark of the northern tribe, but more importantly a sign that he would be a leader.

He grabbed her arm in a blur of motion, pulling her close before she could react.

"Have you seen the living ghost boy?" he asked, his words quick.

She winced in pain from his grasp. "No," she said in his tongue.

He whistled twice, quick fluted sounds. He studied the area around her but maintained his hold.

From either side two more men entered the clearing, dressed like the first but armed with bows. Both had two stripes across their forehead — lower-ranked hunters to the other man.

Grandmother had told her that long ago all people came from one tribe; it was why she treated them equally. Makia did not believe it, though — the northern tribe were ruthless, brutal, and she could not accept that they shared the same blood.

"He is nearby," the first one said. "We can take her as well." He lifted her from the ground.

"Wait," the second one said. "I recognize her. She is the witch's daughter."

The first one let go as if he touched something poisonous. Makia fell back. The third made a sign to ward off evil — something Makia knew was simple superstition. Still they believed it, like they believed many foolish things. It did not make the situation any less deadly for her and others.

"Is this true?" the first one asked.

"I am her granddaughter. Her helper. She sends me into the forest to gather things."

"Witch," the third man said.

"Shasheeni has helped our people a great deal," the second said. "It would be ill fated to harm her blood."

Ghost

"Our people have grown strong. Our shamans provide enough. Find the boy then we can decide what to do with her."

The first kept an eye on her while the other two searched the underbrush. A scurrying erupted behind her. Both men yelled. Makia resisted the urge to look.

There was no need.

The second man carried the boy into the clearing before placing him on the ground. He kept his hand on the boy's shoulder.

The boy cried in hoarse gasps. It was obvious he knew being caught was bad. The third man laughed and the boy cried harder, a wide-mouthed bellow that might have been ear-splitting but for one thing — his tongue had been removed long ago.

His mother had tried protecting him.

Makia longed to comfort the boy. She reached for him but the first jabbed his spear toward her.

"He will not cry for much longer. Tonight we shall roast him, eat him, and we shall have his powers."

Makia's mouth fell open. All three men grinned at this.

"But I think you tried hiding the ghost boy," the first said. "You should come with us."

As he gestured she noticed faint white speckles on his fingers — luminous dots, some of them smeared into fine lines. With a quick glance she saw the same on the others.

They've found a stash of ghost mushrooms.

Not only that but they had pulled them from the stems, and recently. This was one of the rarest of plants, a prize for her grandmother to be used in many ways — sometimes to amplify another plant's effect, other times to counter. But she also knew the care it took to handle them properly, touching only the caps. The stems emitted a fine dust, potent but harmless on its own — but also easily absorbed through the skin, interacting with anything else in your system.

These men knew no such thing; they knew only of greed and taking everything they could.

They should not have touched the stems.

"If you let me go I will give you these." She pulled out several leaves from her pouch, a deep green leaf with thin red veins tracing through it. "Chew these and you shall have a greater strength for many hours." She glanced at the boy. "It will also prepare your body for the eating of a ghost. He is small, but powerful. With this you will be able to take on all of that power."

The first two men exchanged looks; the third kept his eyes on Makia.

"What are these?" the first asked.

"*Sumagoli.* Warrior leaves."

"She should know," the second said.

"They're very rare," Makia said, speaking quickly. "My grandmother would be mad to know I gave the leaves away, but I will give them to you in exchange for my life."

The first lifted them carefully from her palm. He turned them over, inspecting both sides. "If what you say is true I will take them all."

"No!" she said. She needed them all to chew. "That's too much for one person. And they lose their power within a day. But you could each chew one and it will be enough." *It has to be enough,* she thought.

The first man handed a leaf to each. The third held it out before him, his eyes still locked on Makia. She noticed a sack he wore across one shoulder had the same white speckles around the opening — he carried the mushrooms.

"Do not eat the leaves, they are too strong. Chew. Swallow the juices, not the leaves."

The second man sniffed the leaf. He looked at Makia as he put it into his mouth. She smiled at him, nodding as his jaw slowly crushed it.

"It's sweet," he said.

She nodded vigorously.

The first man started chewing his. A hint of a smile reached his eyes. He poked the third man with the blunt end of his spear. "It's good. Chew."

Ghost

The third glanced between Makia and his leader. His distrust of her was evident but his loyalty won out — he too started chewing.

"You will feel the energy very soon. Your running will know no bounds. No one will be able to stand in your way." She smiled with the confidence of knowing she did not lie, though the plant was not as rare as she had said. But it would do as she said and they would return to her grandmother for more — if only they had handled the mushrooms properly.

A big smile broke across the first man's face. He had few teeth left but what he did have were coated in green from the leaf. "You have earned your freedom with this." He hefted the white boy across his shoulder. "I will tell my people to respect your presence in our lands."

These are not your lands, she thought. *Not south of the river.* She had heard similar words from others of the northern tribe. There were too many, and they were not good people.

He turned to the others, his back to her. The boy looked down, his eyes wet with tears and his bottom lip quivering.

She winked at him.

The men disappeared through the woods. They ran with great speed and left little indication of their path. Makia was not a tracker, her skill was in knowing the plants and animals of the forest. She quickly realized the flaw in her plan — if she did not know where they were going she would lose them, they would die on their own, and she would not find her prize.

She ran as fast as she could, crashing through the wild growth like a crazed boar. Her legs tired but she pressed on, the breath burning in her lungs. *It was my only option. They were going to take me too if I didn't do something.* She knew it to be true but it did not make her feel better. Tears stung her eyes as she ran. Knowing what she was losing was too much to bear. A cramp grew in her side but still she pushed.

The ground disappeared before her. In a flurry she grabbed onto a sapling. Clinging with one hand over a drop twice her height, and with the broad river stretching out in front of her, she knew she had lost them.

I'm sorry Grandmother.

Still holding onto the small tree she bent over, easing the cramp and catching her breath. Her tears flowed and her nose ran with snot. As she had often seen Grandmother do she plugged one nostril and blew hard. She turned her head the other way and plugged the other nostril.

A little ways up the river she saw a man fall.

She scurried down the embankment. Staying near the water's edge and as low to the ground as possible she made her way up to where she saw the man.

All three lay on the ground.

The first had fallen, trapping the boy beneath him. He still clutched the spear in his hand. Black froth ran down the side of his mouth. His dilated eyes were shot with blood.

The second had made it to the edge of the river. His head disappeared below the surface, but Makia knew he would otherwise look the same as the first.

The third grunted.

Makia, still standing a short distance away, could not see the man's face but his breathing was obvious. He had not yet died — and may not.

He has the mushrooms.

She knew the man would be weak. She could probably save the boy and get away with him. But this man carried the mushrooms.

As quietly as possible she circled the group, staying behind the heavy growth. The man had not moved and his breath was shallow, but she could now see his face — the sickness had not bubbled from his mouth.

He did not swallow the juice.

The first man was near. The boy struggled to free himself but her eyes went to the spear. She knew she would expose herself going for it, and hoped the man was as weak as he appeared.

Ghost

She ran in five long strides. Grabbing the shaft of the spear she glanced at the third man — his eyes were wide staring straight at her.

He said something, too faint to be understood.

The spear did not budge. She pulled at it furiously but the death grip held firm.

The surviving man pulled a knife from his belt. He rolled over onto all fours.

She pried at the fingers, budging them one at a time.

"Witch," the man said. He had crawled two steps closer.

The spear came free.

She held it in two hands keeping it between her and the crawling man. He *was* weak, but his determination was obvious and her arms quivered. He was a hunter, a warrior, someone who had no-doubt killed countless men. What was she to him?

"Witch!" he said again.

She ran to one side of him. He was slow to follow. With his head turned but his side exposed she drove the spear into his back. She yanked it before he collapsed and jabbed it once more into the side of his neck.

The blood that bubbled from his lips was dark — tainted, but not nearly as poisoned as the others.

The knife had fallen from his hands and she grabbed it. She used it to cut the sack free. It was heavy. Inside was full of mushrooms — stalks and caps. Not all were the ghost mushrooms but many were, far more than she had ever seen.

She rolled the body of the first man off the boy. He had been crying but his face brightened instantly as she helped him to his feet. His smile opened wide once again showing his tongueless mouth.

She took his hand in hers. "You will come home with me," she told him in the southern tongue.

He nodded.

A smile crossed her own face.

LORE

Makia was a bright girl. She knew her grandmother would be ecstatic. She was not only bringing one prize home, but two. *Cooking the ghost boy?* She laughed at their foolish ways.

She knew to gain his powers one must eat him while he still lived.

Dramatis Personae

GEORGE R. GALUSCHAK is a speculative fiction whose work has appeared in over a dozen venues, including *Strange Horizons*, *Ideomancer*, *Escape Pod* and *Space & Time Magazine*. He lives and works in the wilds of northern New Jersey with a ghost cat and a pair of domesticated house plants. A graduate of Viable Paradise and Taos Toolbox, he doesn't have a blog, but you can contact him at galuschak16@gmail.com or @GeorgeGaluschak on Twitter.

TORY HOKE Raised in North Carolina, Tory Hoke now writes, draws, and eats too much sugar-free candy in Los Angeles. She has short speculative fiction forthcoming in *Crowded Magazine* and *Isotropic Fiction*. More of her work can be found at www.thetoryparty.com, including *Meddling Auntie* icebreaker comics for families and a new *Rare Words* vocabulary comic every weekday.

J.J. IRWIN lives in Australia and is a graduate of Clarion South. Her stories have appeared in *Shimmer Magazine*, *Strange Horizons*, and *Andromeda Spaceways*, and she can be found online at deepfishy.livejournal.com and @jj_irwin on Twitter.

S.D. KREUZ lives in Sydney, Australia and has been nurturing her own army of cannibalistic kangaroos, ready to be unleashed as part of her plan for world domination or as a defense force in the event of a zombie apocalypse. She is also spinner of fiction and enjoys bushwalking, archery, and stargazing.

REBECCA M. LATIMER is a Canadian writer of speculative fiction and a recent graduate of the University of Alberta. She is also a part-time visual artist who sometimes illustrates her words. "Robot Time Machines and the Fear of Being Alone" is her first published work of (mostly) fiction.

STEVEN MATHES Steven Mathes has worked with computers for many years. For a short time, he was an expert on the integration of Linux and Windows systems, and wrote a couple of articles for magazines like *Linux Journal*. However, his main interest has always been writing speculative fiction. He has appeared in numerous publications including *Daily Science Fiction, Suddenly Lost in Words,* and *Flash Fiction Online*.

TED MENDELSSOHN is the pen name of Ted Rabinowitz. A graduate of Columbia University and USC's School of Cinema Arts, Ted has also worked as an electrician, speechwriter and professional card player. His first novel, *The Wrong Sword*, was published in 2012; the sequel, *Hero's Army*, will be out next year. He currently lives in New York, where he works as a copywriter and story consultant.

JEFF SAMSON brews Irish stout when he's not writing science fiction and often drinks it when he is. He lives in New Jersey with his wife and little girl, and no cats.

AXEL TORVENIUS has been working as an art director and concept artist in the video game industry for the last eight years. With a background in classic animation, illustration/fine arts, and sculpture, he tries to be as creative as possible in his spare time with different exciting freelance gigs, making sculptures, exploring with his camera, oil paints, t-shirt designs, and album/CD art. His art is often descibed as "dark" or "bizarre," but he doesn't see it in that way. He is simply on a continuous hunt for interesting, emotional, and developing themes, and, most of the time, he is looking for positive feeling. He says, "Even nightmares, however frightening they can be, often leave you with a positive or beautiful aftermath, a sensation that something, even though it was scary at the time, in retrospect, gave you something and meant something. I tend to indulge in themes near or close to death, the occult, and the hidden as often as I can. There is something comforting in shadows."

BEAR WEITER is an illustrator, animator, artist, and writer. His fiction appears in a number of magazines and anthologies including *Black Static*, *Rigor Amortis*, and *Slices of Flesh*. He previously published under the pen names Virginia Ray and Jacob Ruby (which made Ellen Datlow's Honorable Mentions 2012 short list), but he has finally decided to brand everything under one identity — his own. You can follow him on Twitter @bearthw or his personal site: www.bearweiter.com.